P9-AFQ-970

THE SHELTERLINGS

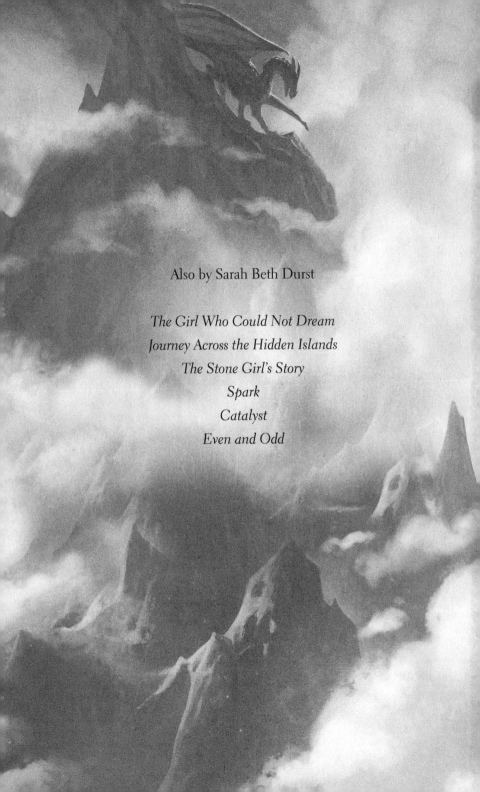

Also by Sarah Beth Durst

The Girl Who Could Not Dream
Journey Across the Hidden Islands
The Stone Girl's Story
Spark
Catalyst
Even and Odd

THE SHELTERLINGS

BY SARAH BETH DURST

CLARION BOOKS
An Imprint of HarperCollins*Publishers*

Clarion Books is an imprint of HarperCollins Publishers.

The Shelterlings

Copyright © 2022 by Sarah Beth Durst

All rights reserved. Printed in the United States of America. No part of this book may be used or reproduced in any manner whatsoever without written permission except in the case of brief quotations embodied in critical articles and reviews. For information address HarperCollins Children's Books, a division of HarperCollins Publishers, 195 Broadway, New York, NY 10007. www.harpercollinschildrens.com

ISBN 978-0-35-835039-2

Typography by Samira Iravani and Marcie Lawrence
22 23 24 25 26   PC/LSCC   10 9 8 7 6 5 4 3 2 1
First Edition

For Noah

CHAPTER ONE

As the only squirrel at the Shelter for Rejected Familiars, Holly always volunteered for the chores that required an exceptionally fluffy tail, such as sweeping the porch.

She hummed to herself as she brushed her tail back and forth. Just a few more strokes and the porch would be spotless. She wanted everything to look as perfect as possible for their new arrival.

Today's arrival would be their first new shelterling since Charlie had left. He used to be the one who greeted the new residents and helped them adjust to their lives at the shelter — he'd been so kind, gentle, and patient with Holly herself when she'd arrived — and Holly wasn't sure she could fill his paws. But she was certainly going to try!

"Gus, can you take the tablecloth off the clothesline before it begins to rain?" she called. "Clover says no one's coming, and it will be sunny all day."

Gus, a barn owl and Holly's best friend, flew out of the upstairs window. He glided on golden-brown wings over the yard. "Whoa, she actually made a useful prediction? She's making progress!"

"I think you were right about the rhyming," Holly said. "It helps her focus." Clover had the power of prophecy, sort of. Her predictions were seldom relevant and always wrong. Holly and Gus had been trying to help her figure out ways to make her prophecies less random.

"Is she getting any better at it?"

"Well, not really, no." The mangled verse that had resulted from their encouraging her to speak in rhyme had made Holly's whiskers twitch, actually. "But she's trying."

Gus landed on the clothesline, and it sagged beneath him. With his beak, he snapped at the clothespins, unhooking them and tossing them onto the lawn. "She was stumped for thirty minutes the other day on a prophecy about an orange."

Holly finished sweeping the porch and shook the dust out of her tail onto the grass. She then scurried around the yard, zigzagging as she gathered up the pins, as well as the few stray leaves and twigs that had fallen since her last cleanup.

"Relax, Holly," Gus said. "It all looks fine. Besides, the new arrival won't care if there's a twig or two out of place. She'll just care that she's coming to a place that is happy to have her. You remember what it was like arriving here after . . . well, *after*."

Stopping, Holly surveyed the yard. It looked better than fine. Lovely, even. The peonies were in full bloom, with plush pink flowers that were twice as big as her head. The house itself — a unique mix of sprawling old farmhouse, barn, and warren — had a fresh coat of white paint with blue trim, and the oversize nest on the porch looked cozy with its pink pillows.

And of course she remembered exactly what it had been like

to arrive at a place she'd never wanted to be. But once you were judged by the wizards as unsuitable to be a familiar, this was where you came and this was where you stayed. The only shelterling to ever leave, so far as Holly knew, had been Charlie, and she still harbored hope that one day he'd come back to stay. Shelterlings lived in the shelter. That was the way it was, and the shelter itself was beautiful. "She's going to love it here," Holly declared.

"Yes, she will."

Shaking out her tail again, Holly trotted back toward the house. The grass tickled her furry stomach. "Did you tell Clover how to rhyme 'orange'?"

"There *is* no rhyme for 'orange.' Anyway, it came out as a prediction about a fruit salad. She rhymed it with 'a mute ballad,' which was brilliant."

Holly hopped up the steps. "She could have used 'door hinge.'"

"That's not . . . Huh, maybe, if you say it fast enough." He flew underneath the tablecloth, lifted it off the line with his head, and carried it draped over his body with his wings sticking out on either side. As he flew into the house beneath the cloth, she heard him muttering, "Orange, door hinge, orange, door hinge," over and over.

She called after him, "Watch out for —"

Thump.

"— the wall," she finished.

"Oops!"

She swallowed a giggle.

"Don't laugh!"

"Of course I wouldn't." She put her tail over her mouth and laughed into the fur as she went inside. She heard a second feathery thump as he bumped into another wall.

"*You* try flying with your eyes blocked."

"You're doing great," she said encouragingly.

Gus reached the dining room at last, settled on the edge of a livestock trough, and shook off the tablecloth. Tugging it with her front teeth, Holly helped him position it over the trough. It wasn't the traditional use of a tablecloth, but she liked how it neatened up the room.

Just because this was a place that no one ever wanted to come didn't mean it couldn't be nice — that was what Charlie used to say, only he'd say "tidy" instead of "nice." Holly had changed it in her head.

She checked the dining room, the front hall, and the living room with its various chairs, couches, and perches for all sizes. Everything felt ready, and her heart thrummed with a little burst of pride. "Do you think the new arrival will like —"

Before she could finish, Zephyr the turtle careened past her. Holly jumped back to keep her paws from being squished. Clinging to Zephyr's shell with all twenty of his sticky toes, Leaf, the gecko who was Zephyr's inseparable best friend, screeched, "Watch out, Holly!"

"Sorry!" Zephyr called.

Holly scooted under a table.

Zephyr skidded as he turned left, bashed into a door frame, and then zoomed on. From the hallway, Leaf squeaked, "Stairs!" And then there was the unmistakable *thump-thump-thump* of a turtle go-ing down a set of stairs very rapidly, followed by a muffled thud as they reached the sublevel of the shelter, where the shelterlings who preferred to live underground had their rooms.

"Are you all right?" Holly called after them.

Zephyr whooped. "That was awesome!"

"That was *not* awesome," Leaf said. "Look at me! Do I look like a gecko who just experienced awesomeness? This is not the face of a happy gecko!"

"But, counterpoint: we only hit half the stairs."

Leaving them to debate the awesomeness or non-awesomeness of their crash, Holly emerged from beneath the table. She exam-ined the doorway where the turtle had hit it. Just a bit of a scuff mark. *I can fix that,* she thought, rubbing it with her tail.

"Holly —" Gus said behind her.

"I know it doesn't have to be perfect," she said. "I just want it to be nice."

"Holly —"

"It's hard enough to summon up the courage to leave your home, only to suffer a huge disappointment," she said. All shelter-lings had once dreamed of becoming familiars, bonded to a wizard and dedicated to a life of making the world a better place. Each of them had left their home, trekked to the very top of Cloud Moun-tain, and drunk from the Moon Mirror — a pool as perfectly round as the moon, which bestowed a magic power on all who drank its waters — and each had then been told by the wizards that the magic the water had given them was small and useless. She scrubbed the doorway harder, as if she could scrub out the memory of that terrible day. "The place you end up should at least be pleasant."

"*Holly.*"

She stopped.

"She's almost here."

"Eeks!" Excited, Holly ran in a circle. "Oh my, oh my." She scurried out the door and down the front walk while Gus glided over her head. He perched on top of the trellis while she peered at the arrival circle, a ring of stones covered in markings known as spell glyphs.

The circle had been created by the original residents of the shelter — the very first shelterlings — with the help of some wizards' familiars. It magically connected the Wizards Tower and the shelter. Like all the shelterlings, Holly had used it when she'd been sent here.

A few of the other shelterlings came outside too, hopping, slithering, and flying to join her and Gus. They all gathered around the arrival circle.

Holly watched as purple sparkles twinkled in the center of the circle. She bounced from paw to paw. It was happening! A new shelterling! Maybe she'd be from a place that Holly had never seen, like an ocean or a desert or a snow-capped mountain . . . Holly used to dream about traveling to new places with her very own wizard, just like Calla, the famous familiar who, in one legend, journeyed with her wizard to a mountain where they saved countless animals from an avalanche with a spell that turned the snow into soap bubbles. In another legend, they trekked deep into a desert to cast a water-summoning spell that created a new oasis.

"I hope she'll be a flamingo," Pepper, a pink flamingo, said. The shelter boasted several birds, but only one flamingo. "Or a pelican. Or a duck. Or a goose. Or a woodpecker. Or —"

One of the resident snakes slithered around the circle of stones. "I hope she'll be a snake. The shelter could use more slithering."

"My heart is set on another mammal," Bluebell said. A lanky, long-eared rabbit, he was wearing his beloved hat, which currently looked like a fedora with holes for his ears. He was the only shelterling who ever wore an accessory — and the only one whose magic worked solely on hats. "Herbivore preferred, please."

The fox next to him bristled. "Carnivores are nice too!"

Within the arrival circle, the sparkles swirled clockwise into a purple cloud. The glyphs on the stones were glowing with a white light that blazed so brightly Holly had to shield her eyes with her tail.

Flying down to land beside her, Gus said to Holly, "Remember my arrival day?"

"I'll never forget it," Holly said. That was the day they'd met. And the day Gus had accidentally crashed through the porch roof while demonstrating his special power. She'd helped him repair it over the next week, and that was how they'd become friends. Well, that and the incident with the acorns.

Her first winter at the shelter, she'd been so very worried all the time — unsettled to be in a new and unexpected place, unsure of her magic, unable to imagine herself in a role other than that of the familiar she'd dreamed of being — and had filled the hall closet with acorns, after she'd finished stuffing her own. No matter how many times Charlie had told her that no rejected familiars were ever sent away from the shelter, she still worried she'd fail here, too. Gus had discovered her extra cache one day while he was exploring; the acorns had tumbled out all over the floor, and Zephyr, practicing his superfast speed, had skidded over them into the dining room, where he'd hit the trough and knocked it over. Unfortunately, it had been full of soup.

Parsnip soup, everywhere.

Gus was the one who had understood. He'd offered up his nest for Holly to store her extra acorns in, no questions asked, until she felt secure enough in her life at the shelter that she didn't need to save quite so many. She'd never forget that kindness. The act of giving up acorn space was the act of a forever friend.

"You're thinking about the parsnip soup, aren't you?" Gus said.

"It went everywhere. Even the ceiling."

"I made the first mess, though, with the porch roof. Of the two disasters, I'd say mine was the more disastrous."

"That all depends on how you feel about parsnip soup," Holly said. She rather liked it. In the forest where she'd grown up, no squirrel ever ate soup. But here, at a place filled with creatures from all over with a variety of different tastes, she'd been able to try soups and breads and cheeses. "We should have made soup for the new arrival."

"We don't even know what kind of animal she is, much less what she'd like to eat. Maybe she doesn't like soup."

"She doesn't like soup?" Bluebell the rabbit said, outraged.

"We don't know," Gus said. "That's my point. We don't know anything about her. We have to wait and see."

They'd been contacted by of one the familiars of Wizards Tower, specifically a badger, who'd said they had a failed applicant. He'd said her name was Periwinkle, but he hadn't mentioned what kind of animal she was, where she was from, or what she was like. Holly thought it was a nice name. She hoped it meant that Periwinkle would be nice herself. Soon they'd find out!

"Deep breath, Holly." Gus demonstrated, inhaling, and his feathers ruffled as he puffed out his chest.

"I'm calm."

"You're vibrating."

Her tail was, in fact, shaking with excitement. She caught it in her forepaws and held it still as the purple sparkles swirled faster and faster. She held her breath.

And then she exhaled, because it was too long to keep holding her breath. She squeezed her tail tighter with both paws. *This is so exciting!* she thought. Whoever this Periwinkle was, she was one of them now: a shelterling.

At last Holly spotted a shape within the purple cloud.

"There she is!" the flamingo cried.

The shape shrieked, and the shelter animals scattered. The rabbit darted behind the hedge, the flamingo flew into the air, the snake slithered into the deeper grass, and the fox jumped away, her ears swept back and her muscles tense.

"I think we're scaring her," Holly said.

"*We're* scaring *her?*" Bluebell said from his hiding place.

Gus flapped his broad wings at the others. "Everyone into the house! Give her some space. Holly will welcome her, and you can all greet her once she's settled in. Shoo, shoo!"

The fox, flamingo, and snake retreated.

"What about you?" Bluebell asked as he hopped toward the porch. His long ears were flattened against his hat.

"Me? I'm just a harmless statue," Gus said, and he held his breath and turned to stone. That was his special power — transforming himself into stone. Granite, to be specific. He looked like and was identical to a lawn ornament, except that he could turn back into flesh-and-blood-and-feathers whenever he liked.

As soon as the others were inside, Holly released her tail and inched closer to the circle of stones. "It's okay," she said gently. "It's just me. My name's Holly."

The purple cloud began to clear, and she saw two huge-as-teacups yellow eyes staring at her. *What are you?* Holly wondered. She'd never seen eyes like that. She saw herself, the Gus statue, the yard, and the house reflected in them. "Your name is Periwinkle, isn't it?"

On all four paws, Periwinkle darted out of the purple sparkles. "You'll never catch meeeeee!" she cried, spurting past Holly. She ducked behind one of the peony bushes.

As Periwinkle ran by, Holly got a much better look at her: a tiny monkey with enormous eyes, framed in triangular black patches, and a black-and-white-ringed tail that was at least two feet long. A lemur! She'd never met a lemur before.

Lemurs lived in the southeast, very far away, in tropical rain-forests that were unlike the meadows, pastures, and oak and pine forests around the shelter. Everything from the temperature to the plants was different. *Ooh, she's going to have so much to tell and so many stories to share, once she settles in,* Holly thought. Rejected familiars didn't travel to faraway lands like familiars did, but hearing about new places was nearly as good as seeing them. She hoped Periwinkle would turn out to be chatty. Holly had dozens of questions.

The last of the sparkles vanished with a *pop-pop-pop*. At the sound, the lemur shrieked and bolted to hide behind the Gus statue.

Gus transformed from a stone statue back into a living owl. "Welcome to the Shelter for Rejected Familiars! So happy to meet you!"

The little lemur shouted, "You can't prove anything! Ha!" and ran under the porch.

"Um, what?" Gus said.

This, Holly thought, *may take a while.*

Soothingly, she said, "That's Asparagus, but we all call him Gus. He's friendly. We're all friendly. Don't worry. Everything is going to be fine."

She heard hoofsteps come around the side of the house and glanced over to see that Clover the cow had wandered into the front yard. She nibbled on the grass and then said, while chewing her cud, "You are absolutely right, Holly. I have foreseen it. Absolutely nothing new will happen. There will be no danger or excitement of any sort. Now that Periwinkle has joined us, everything will be fine. I have so divined."

"Hey, that rhymes!" Gus said. "Fine and divine! Nice job!"

Clover looked delighted. "You're right! I did it!" She repeated her prediction: "Everything will be fine; I have so divined!"

Holly felt her fur stand on end. "That's wonderful, Clover."

Pleased with herself, the cow sauntered off, still chewing.

"You heard Clover," Holly said brightly to the lemur under the porch. "She's gifted with the power of prophecy, and she said everything will be fine."

Behind her, Gus said, "But Holly —"

Don't say it, she thought. *Please, Gus, don't say it.*

"— you know Clover is always wrong."

CHAPTER TWO

Holly sorted through her stash of last fall's acorns — one pile for those with caps and one for those without — while she waited for the lemur. She wanted to be nearby when Periwinkle felt ready to emerge from beneath the porch, but she couldn't just sit still and wait.

Poor thing must be shy, she thought.

When Holly had first arrived, she'd felt as skittish as a baby squirrel. Gathering acorns had been the only thing that made her feel calmer — at least until she became friends with Gus. Charlie had tried to reassure her that it had been similar for the other shelterlings before her. The gecko, Leaf, he'd said, had been so silent and withdrawn when he'd arrived, and it was only when Zephyr joined the shelter that he'd . . . well, not "come out of his shell," since Zephyr was the one with the shell. Pepper had been the opposite. She'd been so wound up when she'd arrived that she'd barely stopped talking for three days. Everyone needed a little help in the beginning, and Holly was determined to be just as patient as Charlie had been with her, even though squirrels weren't typically known for their patience. She'd often wondered if all beavers were as patient as Charlie, or whether he was just special.

Gus amused himself by posing in various positions and then solidifying as a statue: first with both wings outstretched, then one wing up to the sky and the other down, then one leg in the air with his feathers hiked up to show off his knees. Before she'd met Gus, Holly hadn't known that owls even had knees or how surprisingly long their legs were, beneath their feathers. "Hey, Holly, watch this!" He twisted his head 180 degrees, touched the ground with both wings, and hopped — then petrified himself in midair. He stayed like that for three seconds before transforming back into flesh. "Ta-da!"

Holly clapped enthusiastically.

"I'm calling that last move a 'wingstand.'"

"Ooh, try it with acorns," she suggested.

He borrowed two acorns, lifted himself up on his wing tips on top of them, and changed to stone. The acorns cracked beneath his weight. When he turned back to soft feathers, Holly cheered again and claimed the delicious acorn mush.

"Perfectly done," she told him as she nibbled on it. "You're a brilliant talent."

He bowed.

After finishing her snack, Holly lowered her voice and asked, "What do you think Clover's prophecy means? What's going to happen?"

Gus shrugged, which ruffled his feathers. He stuck his beak in between the feathers on his shoulder, neatening them, as he said, "I wouldn't worry too much. Clover's idea of excitement is when someone makes cheese out of her milk."

"Yum. We should make cheese again." It had been a while since they'd had a cheese-making party. Everyone would love it. They'd need to order some of the ingredients from Crescent City, but if they placed an order soon, it would be delivered by train in a few days.

"Mozzarella," Gus said dreamily. "Or ricotta."

"I was thinking cheddar."

"Gorgonzola."

"Definitely not." She gave a little shudder. The smell the one time they'd tried to make gorgonzola cheese had driven half the shelterlings to camp outside for days. She did *not* want to repeat that.

"Manchego. Roquefort. Pepper Jack."

"You just like saying cheese names," Holly teased. "You have no idea what they mean."

Singing the words, Gus said, "Camembert. Gouda. Asiago!"

She sang back, "Cheddar! Brie!"

"Blue cheese! Goat cheese!"

And together: "Feta!"

In a friendly voice, Holly asked, "Periwinkle, what do you like to eat? Fruit? Nuts? You're a prosimian, correct? Primarily plants? Have you ever tried cheese?" She'd never eaten it before she drank from the Moon Mirror and came to the shelter. She knew the same was true for Gus. He was from the Northern Forest, and cheese didn't grow on pine trees. She was from farther west, and they didn't have cheese in their trees either.

From beneath the porch, the lemur shouted, "You can't trick me with all your cheese talk!"

Maybe not shy, Holly thought. *But definitely confused.*

"No tricks here," Gus said cheerfully. "Just food."

"Do you like fruit?" Holly asked. "Strawberries are in season, and we have an excellent strawberry patch. Would you like to see it?"

"Absolutely not," Periwinkle said. "I am staying right here until you promise that I won't be punished in any way."

Holly glanced at Gus, and he shrugged his feathery shoulders.

"What would we punish you for?" Holly asked.

"Uh . . . nothing." Her voice was muffled, as if she'd crawled even farther back beneath the porch. Peering under, Holly couldn't even see the reflection of the lemur's eyes.

"Why would you think we'd want to?" Gus asked.

"No reason," came the reply.

Why would she think . . . *Oh!* Holly thought. *I understand. At least I think I do . . .* Gently, she said, "You weren't sent here as a punishment."

Gus chimed in. "The familiars and their wizards should have made that clear before they did their purple smoke trick." He glared back at the arrival circle, as if it had been rude. "This isn't a prison. It's a haven for animals like us."

"That's not what they say when they think no one's listening."

Periwinkle's voice was slightly less muffled, as if she'd crept closer to the yard. "This is a place they send animals they want to forget about. And yes, I eavesdropped, and I'm not sorry."

"The shelter is *not* a punishment," Holly said as firmly as she could. "You didn't do anything wrong. You just . . ." *Failed*, she thought, but she didn't want to say that out loud. "The wizards didn't have a place for you."

"They called me useless," Periwinkle said. "They said I was a mistake."

Holly winced. They'd said that about her, too. She wished they'd be kinder when they leveled their judgment. It wasn't as if any of the shelterlings had chosen to only be able to do silly parlor tricks. All of them had expected to be gifted with the kind of magic that would have made them the next Ash, the familiar who'd helped his wizard transform a rampaging basilisk into a friendly kitten, or Emerald, the familiar who'd used an ice spell with her wizard to stop a forest fire. Now *that* was real magic.

"You're in good company," Gus said cheerfully. "We've all been called mistakes here." He tilted his head to peer under the porch. "But we're also friendly, and we have delicious soup. So there's no need to be shy. Why don't you come on out, and we'll show you around?"

Holly waited, thinking that Periwinkle would finally emerge, but she didn't.

"You must be hungry from your ordeal," Holly said. "I'll get you some strawberries." She scurried around the house to the back, where the berries grew. She loved the shelter's gardens. They had a vegetable garden where they grew carrots, radishes, lettuce, and corn, as well as a strawberry patch and a pumpkin patch. On the other side of the vegetables, closer to the pasture, they also had an orchard with peach trees, apple trees, and pecan trees. Everyone took turns planting and harvesting — unless you chose to forage for your own food beyond the shelter grounds. Those were the rules, and they made life at the shelter both fair and pleasant.

Really, it was wonderfully pleasant, for a place that no one wanted to be.

No one ever dreamed of becoming a shelterling. Most never even knew it was possible to drink from the Moon Mirror and fail to become a familiar — Holly certainly hadn't known. It wasn't common. Not many creatures made the trek to the top of Cloud Mountain in the first place. Really, only a few a year. Some years one or two became shelterlings; some years none did.

Holly was the only squirrel she knew who had left her tree and her acorn caches and journeyed to the Moon Mirror. She'd wanted to be a familiar so badly. Being a familiar . . . it meant a life of adventure. And of purpose. If you didn't want to live the same life as your parents, siblings, cousins, and neighbors, then becoming a familiar was the best option for changing things. You could leave your forest or field or prairie and be welcomed with open arms into a brand-new, exciting life as a wizard's sidekick, traveling from place to place, wherever magical help was needed . . . or at least that was the way it was supposed to happen.

She'd journeyed to the top of Cloud Mountain and drunk from

the Moon Mirror. Like all the others who'd done the same, she'd gained her own unique power, and she'd presented herself to the wizards. And then . . .

Holly didn't like to think about what had happened next.

As she picked the plumpest strawberries, she made a mental list of who she should introduce Periwinkle to first, if the lemur ever emerged from beneath the porch. She could start with the smaller shelterlings, then work her way up to larger animals. She'd save the carnivores for last, even though they all had very nice manners. There was no reason for any herbivore to fear any carnivore at the shelter. Everyone was well-fed, either with produce from the garden or kibble shipped in by train from the cities, depending on their palate. It wasn't like being out in the wild. *We're all friends here,* Holly thought. No shelterling would ever do anything to hurt another shelterling. But it might take a while for her to convince their new arrival of that. *I'll need to be patient.*

With her arms full of strawberries, she waddled back to the front of the house. It wasn't easy to walk on her hind legs like a human — squirrels weren't designed for it — but she'd had practice, using her tail for balance. She felt a bit ridiculous, but if the strawberries helped make Periwinkle feel welcome, it would be worth it.

Holly deposited them in front of the porch. "Are you hungry?"

A little handlike paw shot out, snagged a strawberry, and then disappeared back underneath.

That's a start, Holly thought.

She glanced around, looking for Gus, but she didn't see him.

Sitting on the grass near the porch, Holly tried to think of what to say that would coax their new arrival out. In a friendly tone, she asked, "Where are you from?"

"Rainforest."

"Did you like it there?"

"No."

Of course the answer was no. The lemur wouldn't have left her rainforest home and gone to all the effort to drink from the Moon Mirror if she'd been happy with her life. Holly swatted herself with her tail for asking such a silly question. "You might like it here, if you give it a chance. It's a nice place."

"I don't want to be here."

"Maybe you could try? You might *grow* to like it here."

Muffled again, the lemur said, "You might not like me."

Aw, that was sweet! Holly had never met anyone who worried about whether she'd like them. She liked everyone. Or at least she tried to. "Of course we'll like you! Why wouldn't we?" Holly inched closer and tried to make her voice as warm and reassuring as possible.

"The other lemurs, they used to call me a pest. An annoying bother that no one wanted, they said. I wasn't obedient enough, they said. I wouldn't just do as I was told. I was always asking questions. I was always in the way. I just wanted to know *why* I was supposed to obey. Things were supposed to be better after I drank the magic water — but it turned out the wizards didn't want me either. They said that I'm 'unsuitable.' And that I steal stuff."

Poor Periwinkle, Holly thought. She knew what rejection felt like. She'd been so excited at first after she'd gained her power, but the wizards . . . they'd judged her unsuitable too. "Well, that wasn't very nice of them to say. You don't steal. Do you?"

In a tiny voice, Periwinkle said, "Yes."

For an instant, Holly was speechless. She thought maybe she'd heard her wrong. "You . . . you do? Um, maybe you could just . . . not do that?"

"I won't."

"Good." Holly felt her fur settle. "Wait — when you say 'I won't,' do you mean you won't steal or you won't *not* steal?" She hid her acorn stash under her tail. She wouldn't like anyone touching her cache, and she knew several of the other animals, especially the rodents, felt the same about their winter hoards.

"See? You aren't going to like me. No one ever likes me. I'm a pest and a thief."

She wondered what exactly the lemur had done — or what the wizards *thought* she'd done. "Did you steal from the wizards?"

"No." And then: "Yes. Maybe. I took their dumb test. When they asked me to demonstrate my power, I showed them all their lost stuff that I'd found. And they said I stole it. But I didn't. I *found* it."

Holly wasn't sure what Periwinkle meant by "found," but at the very least the lemur could have a fresh start at the shelter. "Well, um, have you stolen anything here yet?"

A paw stuck out from under the porch. It was holding a clothespin.

Holly took it. She must have missed this one when Gus had

plucked them off the line. It had probably rolled under the porch. "Thank you. I don't think it counts as stealing if you're finding and returning an item I lost."

Periwinkle poked her head out from under the porch. Her black nose was wet like a dog's, and her eyes were bright yellow. "It doesn't?"

Firmly, Holly said, "It doesn't. So long as you don't keep what doesn't belong to you, you're helping, not hurting anyone." She held herself still so that the lemur wouldn't disappear again. "I'm glad you found it. I hadn't even known I'd lost it."

"I . . . that's what I can do now, my special power that the water gave me." The lemur crept out farther onto the lawn. "I can find things. Little things that someone lost, or that aren't where they're supposed to be. It's like I see this shimmery glow out of the corner of my eye, and if I follow it, it gets brighter and brighter until I pick up whatever it is. And then it shines like the sun. I can't resist it. It's so pretty that I have to have it! And why shouldn't I? Its owner didn't want it. Its owner lost it. But I found it. I rescued it! Like the clothespin." She stretched out her paws, and Holly passed it back to her. The lemur cradled it in her arms lovingly. "I saw its glow, and I found it and treasured it and saw how beautiful and special it was. Somebody made this, and you didn't even know it was missing. You didn't care! I did!" By the end of her speech — her longest one yet — she was glaring at Holly as if she expected the squirrel to scold her.

"I think that's a lovely power to have," Holly said. The lemur was right — she hadn't missed the clothespin or ever thought of it as beautiful. It was rather charming that Periwinkle saw it that way, as treasure. That didn't make her a thief. "Your power is much better than mine."

The lemur continued to glare, but she asked, "What's yours?"

"I'll show you, but please don't laugh." Holly squeezed her eyes and concentrated. Her fur tingled from the top of her head all the way down her tail. Her ears began to itch. And then she heard a popping sound.

In her paws, Holly held a moon-shaped roll of flaky dough. "Um, what's that?"

"It's called a croissant," Holly said. She scooted closer so the lemur could sniff it. It smelled as fresh as if it had come from an oven. The pads of her paws felt warm as she held it, and she knew she'd have to lick off the excess butter. "I can conjure pastries."

"But . . . you're a squirrel. Shouldn't you conjure acorns?" Periwinkle gestured at Holly's piles of capped acorns and capless acorns.

"Yes, that would be a useful power," Holly said, "but this is all I can do. Croissants, muffins, buns, cinnamon rolls, donuts . . . I can vary the kind of pastry, but it's always only a pastry." Every time she talked about it, she wanted to curl into a ball of embarrassment and hide inside a tree for an entire season. It was an utterly ridiculous power. Even if the pastries were delicious. "You said the wizards didn't want you. Well, they laughed at me."

The test to become a familiar was a three-day ordeal. On the first day, the wizards taught the applicant how to pronounce the basic glyphs, the symbols in the ancient language of wizardry that they used to write out their spells, and the applicant would try to cast several simple spells — any animal who had drunk from the Moon Mirror usually succeeded at that task, she'd heard. Holly remembered how proud she'd been at the beginning. But then, on the second day, the applicant was asked to demonstrate their own special power. They were given a series of challenges and told to solve them using only their magic. She'd had to open a puzzle box, navigate a maze in the dark, and retrieve a key from the roof of the Wizards Tower. Croissants and muffins had been no help at all. On the third day, she'd faced the wizards, and they'd delivered their judgment: *You have a useless power*, they'd told her. None of them had wanted her as their familiar. She'd tried and failed to conjure anything but baked goods, and they'd laughed so hard that some of them had cried.

But that was the past. Right now, she'd rather concentrate on helping a new arrival who clearly needed some cheering up. *That* was something she could do without any special power. "Come inside," Holly coaxed. "I promise you're going to like it here, and everyone is going to like you."

She continued to hold out the croissant.

"You can't promise that," Periwinkle said.

"I can promise we'll all try," Holly said.

Warily, Periwinkle took it and, nibbling on the pastry, followed Holly inside.

CHAPTER THREE

"No one likes her, Holly," Gus said.

Holly flopped her tail over her head. "I know."

It had been three days since the lemur had arrived, and every day was worse than the one before. She'd managed to alienate or irritate nearly everyone.

"What did she do now?" Holly asked, muffled by fluff. "Wait, don't tell me. Let me enjoy not knowing." Half a minute later, she began to feel silly. She lowered her tail, summoned her courage, and said, "Okay, tell me."

"She took Bluebell's hat," Gus said.

Holly winced. While it was admittedly unusual for a rabbit to have a hat, Bluebell was very attached to his. That may have been the very worst item in the whole shelter for Periwinkle to "rescue." *Not that Periwinkle would know that,* Holly thought. *It could be an innocent mistake.*

Or not.

She sighed. Maybe Charlie would have known what to do with a new shelterling like Periwinkle, but she didn't. She wasn't a natural leader like Charlie, or a familiar with a wizard who always knew the right spell to cast in any situation. She was just a little squirrel who conjured croissants and muffins.

But she couldn't just turn away if there was a chance she could help. *I have to try,* she thought. Periwinkle was here for good, and they were all just going to have to find a way to get along. "I'll talk to her. And him."

"You might want to start with him," Gus suggested. "He's in the kitchen, and he's gotten into the blueberry jam. He'll listen to you." Under his breath, he added, "Certainly didn't listen to me."

She heard him and stopped, halfway to the kitchen. "Asparagus, was he mean to you?" Gus was the nicest owl in the entire world, and if Bluebell had lashed out —

"Of course not. He's just melodramatic. You know how he gets."

She studied his heart-shaped face to make sure he wasn't upset, but Gus seemed fine. He was his usual unflappable self. "I'll try, but I don't know if he'll listen to me any better than he did to you." With that, she headed into the kitchen.

Sprawled across the top of the table, his long ears hanging over the edge, was Bluebell the rabbit. He was singing to himself in a doleful voice, "Oh, glorious hats! Glorious, glorious hats! Bowlers and beanies, caps and fedoras, berets and bonnets, boaters and turbans . . . Oh, glorious hats for me." His voice hitched. "No hat for me."

She climbed up the table leg to reach him. Jam was smeared all over the rabbit's mouth, whiskers, and belly fur. He even had a dab of blueberries on his cotton tail. "Bluebell? Are you all right?"

He draped his front paw dramatically over his face. "I most emphatically am not. I'm miserable, Holly. No, that word doesn't go far enough. I am despondent. I am forlorn! I am bereft of joy!"

"Bluebell . . ."

"And bereft of *my hat*."

"Bluebell, where's your hat?"

He let out a sob.

It was pointless to talk to him when he got like this. No wonder Gus had had no luck. The wonder was that Gus had thought she'd fare any better. She tried a more specific question. "Does Periwinkle have your hat?"

He began to moan.

"I'll ask Periwinkle about your hat. You wait here, and please don't eat any more jam. You're going to make yourself sick." She hurried down the table leg and out of the kitchen.

On her way up the stairs, she spotted the shelter's resident porcupine, Tangerine, trying to hide. Again. His special gift was camouflage — or at least he said it was. Holly had only ever seen him turn the opposite color of whatever he stood near: purple against a yellow door, red against blue sky, polka dots against plaid. He kept trying, though.

She politely pretended she didn't see him, despite the fact that his quills and fur were a brilliant orange against the green wallpaper.

As she passed, she heard him whisper to himself, "Yay!"

Pepper the flamingo waltzed out of her room. "Hi, Holly. Hi, Tangerine."

And the porcupine whispered to himself, "Boo."

"Good morning, Pepper," Holly said. In as cheerful a voice as she could, she said, "Tangerine, I nearly didn't see you!"

"Humph," the porcupine said before waddling into his room.

Well, it was worth a try, she thought.

Pepper twisted her neck, pretzel-like. "Oh! I didn't mean . . . Tangerine, I'm sorry!" To Holly she said, "I didn't mean to hurt his feelings. I didn't know he was practicing."

It was admittedly hard to tell, since the porcupine never actually succeeded in blending in. "It's good that he tries."

"Is it?" Pepper asked. "I'm not sure. The harder he tries, the more he contrasts. He looked more orange than I am pink." She fluttered her pink wings as evidence. "He'd be happier if he stopped trying so hard. I mean, it's not like he *needs* to be able to camouflage. He's already got quills."

Loudly, from his room, Tangerine said, "Ordinary porcupines use their quills. I don't want to be ordinary. That was the whole point of going to Cloud Mountain in the first place."

Pepper winced. "Oops. I didn't think he was still listening."

Before the flamingo could stick her foot in her mouth — or, more accurately, beak — again, Holly conjured a muffin and held it up to her. "Brine shrimp–flavored."

"Aw, thanks, Holly. And sorry again, Tangerine!" Pepper took the muffin with her curved beak and then flew downstairs and out the window.

Calling through Tangerine's doorway, Holly said, "If you'd like to practice with me later, just let me know." She'd try to think of more exercises that could get him closer to blending in. Maybe Gus would have some new ideas.

When Tangerine didn't reply, she left his favorite kind of éclair outside his door, in hopes it would cheer him up, and continued on to the end of the hall.

Every shelterling had his or her own space — the shelter was sprawling enough for that. Some lived in tunnels beneath the house, some lived in stalls in the attached barn, and some had rooms within the former farmhouse.

Years ago, before Holly's time, the shelter had been started by a group of rejected familiars, the first shelterlings, who had taken over an abandoned farm. Through the years, they'd fixed the house up and added onto it, making it much more suited to birds, reptiles, and mammals of all sizes. Periwinkle's room had been a nursery before it was converted to a chicken roost and then a substitute rainforest.

Outside the door, Holly called, "Periwinkle? It's me, Holly. Are you in there?"

"No," she heard.

Holly went inside.

Periwinkle's room was draped in ribbons. Mimicking vines, they hung from the ceiling, from the top of the window, from the lamps, and from the bed frame. Marveling at the sight, Holly ducked under a strip of white linen. She wondered where the little lemur had found so many ribbons . . . but that wasn't what she was here to ask. She peered around, looking for the lemur. In one corner she found a pile of broken bits of glass. In another were sunflower seeds. In another were screws, nails, and bolts. *She's been busy,* Holly thought, *rescuing her treasures.* And in the fourth corner was Periwinkle, with what looked like a fedora in her paws.

"Periwinkle?"

The lemur jumped.

"Is that Bluebell's hat?"

She clutched it tighter. "No."

Holly tried again, making an effort to channel Charlie's patience. "Do you own a hat?"

"Now I do."

Why was Periwinkle like this? It was one thing to keep bits of glass that no one wanted, but she had to see there was a difference between unwanted items and Bluebell's hat. Holly reminded herself to speak calmly. "Where did you find it?"

"Under the stairs," Periwinkle said. "It was lost. It had the glow."

It was entirely possible that Bluebell had hidden it and lost track of where, which did make it technically a lost item. She supposed she could understand how Periwinkle had made such a mistake. It wasn't that she *meant* to steal. "He hides it to keep it safe whenever he isn't wearing it. Why didn't you return it when you learned who it belonged to?"

"Because he didn't appreciate it. He wouldn't have lost it if he did."

"You can't keep it," Holly said.

"Why not? I'll take better care of it than he did."

She was certain that Periwinkle knew perfectly well why she

couldn't keep it. Yesterday she'd "found" a cache of dried berries that belonged to the skunk, Strawberry, who'd misplaced them beneath a couch cushion. She'd told Strawberry that if she didn't value them enough, then she shouldn't get to eat them. And the lemur had popped them into her mouth right in front of the skunk, as if daring her to spray.

Strawberry, who hadn't sprayed once since coming to the shelter, had demonstrated exactly what her power was. She'd looked straight at Periwinkle, and the lemur's nose had wrinkled.

"They taste like mud," the lemur had said, around her mouthful.

"Then spit them out," Strawberry had said.

Periwinkle hadn't.

A second later she'd wrinkled her nose again and said, "Ugh, swamp-flavored."

"I can change the smell of anything," Strawberry said. "And smell and taste are linked." As Periwinkle moved to leave the room, the skunk called after her, "It's not too late — you can still spit them out."

Periwinkle had swallowed.

Later, Holly had asked Periwinkle why she had done it.

The lemur had shrugged and said, "She didn't like me anyway."

This time, since it didn't look likely that Periwinkle was going to eat Bluebell's hat, Holly said, "You know, it's possible you'd make friends faster if you'd stop taking everyone's stuff."

Periwinkle said, "I told you. I found it."

"You'll make friends faster if you *return* the stuff you find."

"Doubt it," Periwinkle said. "The wizards were very certain. I'm a thief."

Holly considered the lemur's words. "You aren't a thief," Holly said staunchly. "You're — you're a *new collector* who sometimes, because of your lack of experience as a collector, makes mistakes."

Wide-eyed, Periwinkle stared at her, and Holly could tell she was thinking about that. "I'm a collector." She said the word slowly, as if trying it out.

"A collector who sometimes makes mistakes *and* can fix them, if she wants to." Holly held out her paw. *Come on, Periwinkle,* she thought. *Be reasonable.* "We all have to live together, so it's important we all try to be nice to one another."

Periwinkle hugged the hat again, and the brim bent in her paws. "They're not nice to me," she said in a low voice.

Holly wished the other shelterlings could see Periwinkle like this. She wasn't malicious or even mischievous. She was scared. She'd been misunderstood by everyone she met for a very long time — first the other lemurs calling her a pest just for using her brain, and then the wizards calling her a thief just for using her power. It must be hard to believe you were good when so many told you over and over that you weren't. "I've been nice to you, haven't I?" Certainly she'd been trying.

Reluctantly, Periwinkle said, "Yes."

"Then, as a way of being nice to me, come with me to the kitchen, return Bluebell's hat, and apologize. Will you do that for me? Please?"

The lemur's eyes seemed even larger than they'd been the other day, but she inched forward, with the hat. "Why are you still nice to me?"

"Because I want you to be happy here," Holly said.

"You do?"

"Please, Periwinkle, come with me, apologize to Bluebell, and set things right."

The lemur followed her down to the kitchen, and Holly coaxed her through her apology. Several times Periwinkle darted off mid-sentence and returned with an item that had undoubtedly been lost at some point — a piece of string, a cap to a jar, a sponge, a sliver of soap — but at last she got through the words, and the hat was restored to Bluebell's head.

"Oh, glorious hat for me!" Bluebell sang as he patted the fedora, and in a puff of sparkly smoke it transformed into a wide-brimmed hat with a fake flower on its ribbon.

Periwinkle gasped and whispered, "I should have kept that hat."

"It's not a magic hat," Holly told her. "It's just a hat. Bluebell is the one with magic. He can change any hat into any other kind of hat. That's his gift from the Moon Mirror."

Lovingly, Bluebell curled the ribbon into a bow.

Holly continued. "But, magic or not, he really does love his hat, even if he misplaced it."

Suddenly, Bluebell let out a high-pitched yelp, and Periwinkle—saying "uh-oh"—bolted out of the kitchen. Holly asked Bluebell, "What's wrong now?"

"There's jam on the ribbon! And it's all her fault! If she hadn't taken my hat . . ."

"It's not *all* her fault. You ate the jam. Messily. Let me see." She peered at the ribbon, which had blueberry jam smeared across the silk. She didn't know anything about stains, except that you were supposed to soak the fabric in either cold or hot water, and —

From the other room, she heard a crash, and she jumped. "Eeks! Is everyone okay?" As Bluebell launched into another mournful song, she hurried into the living room.

Zephyr was upside down, spinning in a circle on his shell with his stubby legs flailing in the air. Leaf was bouncing around the room, literally. He'd puffed up like a balloon and was ricocheting off the walls and ceiling. That was his power — to inflate in a floating sphere — but he hated floating, so it usually only happened by accident, when he was startled. Like now. The turtle must have crashed again, but why —

She spotted the cause:

All over the floor were dozens of acorns.

"My acorns!" Holly cried. Zigzagging through the room, she gathered up as many acorns as she could in her front paws. She'd thought she'd hidden these! She chittered, hugging an armful to her chest, before asking, "What happened?"

Spinning, Zephyr pointed with his front leg.

Unfortunately, since he was spinning, that meant he was pointing everywhere.

"Yes, I see the acorns." He must have careened into the living room at his usual top speed, with Leaf on his back, and slipped on them. Leaf must have gotten scared and swelled into a floating ball, and that must have been what led to the sight before her, with all her beautiful acorns sprawled everywhere. "They must have . . ." She trailed off, not knowing how the acorns could have gotten out of the closet under the stairs where she'd stashed them. She'd latched the door, or at least she thought she had. Was this her fault?

"Not the acorns," Zephyr said. "*Her*."

She finally saw what he was trying to point at, or more accurately *who*. Tucked underneath an armchair was a little lemur. "Periwinkle?"

Laughing, the lemur rolled onto her back and kicked her paws in the air. "Did you see — he just — spun and spun — and — ha!"

"At least no one was hurt," Holly said, trying to find any bit of good in this mess. She began loading the acorns back into the closet, sweeping them inside with her tail. She didn't remember how many she'd had in this particular cache. She hoped none had rolled outside. It had taken weeks of work to gather this many, and while she didn't truly *need* a cache anymore, it was still hers. Out in the woods, other squirrels raided caches all the time, but she'd never imagined that here —

From upstairs, she heard Pepper shout, "Anyone seen my mollusk?"

All of them — Holly, Zephyr, and Leaf — looked at Periwinkle.

The lemur fled up the staircase, shouting, "You see, everyone blames me even when it *isn't* my fault! Even you, Holly! You think I'm trouble too! But I didn't take it! You can't prove it! And you can't catch meeeeeee!"

Holly was about to follow her when Gus called from outside, "Holly!"

Now what? she thought.

"Holly! Come to the front yard! Come see who's here!"

Another emergency? she worried.

But Gus sounded excited, not alarmed. Maybe this was a good interruption, not a third disaster in a row. Please? Hoping for the best, she left Zephyr, Leaf, and her beloved acorns and hurried out the door onto the porch.

Gus was gliding above a beaver — a very familiar beaver, with white whiskers and a thick paddle-like tail that dragged behind him as he strolled up the front walk. He was carrying a leather satchel with a diagonal strap across his furry chest.

Could it be? Really?

Holly stared for a moment longer, and then she ran, picking up speed, before launching herself at the beaver and landing in the soft fuzz of his belly. "Charlie!"

Laughing, he cradled her in a hug before setting her back down. He waved one of his front paws, and a bouquet of lilacs popped into existence. Bending down to her level, he presented them to her. "A thank-you for the warm welcome, to the loveliest squirrel of all."

"It's wonderful to see you, Charlie!" She had a thousand questions: Where had he gone, why had he returned, and was he here to stay? He'd come back! This was amazing! It was as if a wish she hadn't even thought to make had been miraculously granted.

"You too, my friend," he replied.

Hugging the flowers, she inhaled the sweet smell of lilacs. After everything with Periwinkle . . . Charlie coming back was the best thing that could have possibly happened. She felt as if a hundred worries had been lifted off her shoulders. How had he known to come, just when she needed him?

He's exactly the animal to set things right, she thought. He could help Periwinkle settle in, convince her to leave everyone's personal property alone, and coax the others into forgiving their new arrival's . . . quirks. After all, every one of them had quirks. That was, in truth, why they were here. "Please say you're back for good!"

Charlie laughed his jovial belly laugh. "I missed you, too."

Gus flew to the upper windows of the house. "Hey, everyone! Charlie's back!"

Hearing him, Zephyr, with Leaf on his back, zipped out of the house and across the lawn. "Charlie! Yay! Welcome home!" the turtle cried before he crashed into a bush.

Leaf scolded his friend for not slowing down.

Watching them fondly, Charlie said, "Ah, delightful how little changes."

She wanted to tell him there *had* been changes. Holly had been helping Breeze the bat practice turning invisible — when Charlie had left, he could only turn half of himself invisible, but now he could vary which half. Clover had been adding rhymes to her prophecies and was showing signs of improvement. Sparkles the duck, who exuded sparkles whenever she flapped her wings, had laid her first egg, and it had had a sparkly shell. One of the mice, Marble, had "accidentally" eaten a hole in the living room carpet and used the fibers to help the robin Ivy finish building her nest. Two of the snakes had molted. But Charlie had switched his attention to Bluebell.

"Ho, Bluebell!" Charlie said. "Still with the hat, I see."

On the porch, Bluebell swept his hat in a dramatic circle. "Indeed! Welcome home, dear friend! We feared the worst. A treacherous journey. A terrible storm. Unfriendly foes."

Actually, we didn't know what to think, Holly thought. None of them had known where he'd gone or when he'd planned to return. Charlie had only said he'd had "questions that needed answering." He hadn't said anything more, and no one had been able to convince him to stay.

But he's back now, she thought, *and that means everything's going to be all right.*

Pepper flapped her wings as she settled onto the lawn. "Charlie, where have you been? Beavers aren't supposed to migrate. But since you did travel . . . where did you go? What did you see? Did you meet any interesting birds? Don't spare any details. We want to know what you saw, heard, smelled —"

"Did you find yourself in danger?" Bluebell chimed in. "Are you hurt? An unseen wound? Why have you returned? Have you come to warn us of some unforeseen disaster?" He posed dramatically, with his hat obscuring his face.

Charlie held out his paws and made a calming gesture. "All is well. And I promise I'll tell you everything — where I've been, what I've done, and why I've returned. But what I have to say needs to be heard by all shelterlings, most especially your newest arrival."

"Periwinkle?" Holly asked, surprised.

"Watch your stuff around her," Leaf warned, with a meaningful look at Charlie's satchel. The beaver laid his paw over the clasp.

Bluebell held up his hat, which was now a top hat with a blueberry smear on the brim. "She took my most prized possession!"

"She just . . . hasn't fully settled in yet," Holly said. "Charlie, do you mean to say you know about her?" It wasn't a secret when animals failed to become familiars, but it wasn't shouted from the rooftops, either.

"Know about her? She's the reason I came back!" Charlie said. "I need her help."

"*Periwinkle?*" Bluebell said, aghast.

Charlie nodded. "I believe she may be the key to changing our lives."

CHAPTER FOUR

With his satchel next to him, Charlie had claimed his old seat in the living room, a beat-up comfy chair with patches and a leg-rest, and was waiting patiently for the other shelterlings to assemble. Every inch of carpet in front of him was occupied by someone furry, feathered, or scaled. The shelter had twenty residents — twenty-two now that Periwinkle had arrived and Charlie had come back — but they rarely gathered all together like this, due to their different habits. Holly fidgeted with her tail fluff while the other shelterlings shifted and scooted until everyone had found a spot to sit, coil, or perch. The fox let one of the mice sit on her head for a better view. The other mouse crawled up onto the light fixture to keep the bat company. The skunk and the porcupine were sharing a couch pillow. The snakes occupied one corner of the carpet, in an interwoven coil. The flamingo stood behind them, her wings folded and one leg tucked underneath her. Everyone was here. Even the cow, Clover, who never liked to come inside, had stuck her head in through an open window.

Their newest shelterling poked her pointy face around the door frame.

"Ah, you must be Periwinkle!" Charlie boomed.

Periwinkle shrieked, "I didn't do it!" and withdrew her nose from view.

Holly sighed inwardly.

"Don't be scared, little one," Charlie called after her. "I've traveled a long way to meet you. My name is Charlie." He paused, as if expecting her to reply, but she didn't answer and didn't reappear. He continued as if she had. "I like to keep an ear open for what's happening, and when a friend of mine told me about your experience with the wizards and their lack of appreciation for your talent . . . well, let's say I appreciate you."

"She's . . ." Holly began. She wanted to use the word "shy," but it was more like "prickly." The lemur was so convinced that everyone would dislike her that she pushed them away before they even had a chance to try. Picking her words carefully, Holly said, "She's still getting used to being here."

"But she's listening." Charlie winked at her.

He didn't seem at all upset by Periwinkle's behavior. That was Holly's favorite thing about Charlie: his unfailing patience. He'd been patient with her when she'd been an anxious new arrival — she'd scurry through the shelter at all hours, gathering and storing her acorns, but each night when she finished, she'd find him in the kitchen, brewing tea for her. He'd made Holly feel welcome, and she knew he'd do the same for Periwinkle. *Very lucky he heard about her,* Holly thought, though she still wanted to know *why* that had prompted him to return. "You said she was the key to changing our lives. What did you mean by that?"

"Is everyone here?" Charlie said. "What I have to say affects all shelterlings."

Gus counted from his perch on the back of one of the chairs. "All here."

"Very well, then," Charlie said. "My explanation begins, as all important things do, with a story, specifically 'The Tale of the Moon Mirror.'"

"Ooh, I love this story," one of the mice cheered. Others chimed in too.

The fox hushed the mouse, who hushed the bat, who hushed the flamingo and the toad . . . and so on. As they all settled down, Holly saw movement out of the corner of her eye. The lemur was creeping along the wall of the living room. Her eyes were fixed on Charlie's chair. No one else was paying any attention to her, but Holly watched without moving, the way she used to watch predators in the woods from up in her tree. She was capable of holding still when she wanted to. Not as still as Gus when he turned to stone, but fairly still.

Periwinkle darted under Charlie's chair.

She wondered if Charlie knew Periwinkle was there. She suspected he did. When he'd been a resident at the shelter, he'd been aware of everything happening under the roof and had excelled at soothing rattled nerves and solving disputes. No one had been able to fill his paws after he'd left. Who could? This was *Charlie.*

He began. "Long, long ago, so long that our trees were mere acorns and our rivers were undammed, there was a group of animals —"

"At least one of them was a bird," Pepper the flamingo said. "I heard one version that said it was an osprey and another that said it was a wren."

"There was definitely a cow," Clover said from the window. "I have seen it in my dreams: a cow, or so it seems. Ooh, Gus, how was that one?"

"Very nice," Gus said. "Or you could go with 'a cow made it supreme.'"

"I have seen it in my dreams: a cow made it supreme!"

Charlie held up his paw. "History has been lost to myth. We don't know which animals were present, but we do know that these animals wanted different lives from the ones they had. They wanted magic and adventure. But in those days, there was no magic within animal-kind."

"Or bird-kind," Pepper said.

Others hushed her.

Charlie continued. "You have heard how these creatures climbed to the top of the highest peak of our land, within the clouds, and cast a spell to create the magic pool known as the Moon Mirror. Anyone who chooses to drink from this water is gifted with a unique power. But what you have not heard is *how* our ancestors achieved such a feat."

Holly crept closer, between the marmot and the robin. "You discovered this?"

"I did." He smiled at her. "During my travels, I have been chasing the truth. Bits of stories, of myths, of memories, all to discover the true source of our magic. And at last, after much painstaking research, I know how it all began."

It was quiet in the living room.

"Those long-ago animals gathered seven special magical ingredients for their spell and carried them to the top of Cloud Mountain. There, close to the sun, the moon, and the stars, they cast a spell, all of them speaking together as one."

"What ingredients?" Zephyr asked, transfixed.

"Was one a hat? A glorious hat?" Bluebell asked.

Charlie beamed at them as he opened his satchel and withdrew a notebook. With his claws, he flipped pages. "What ingredients — that is the key, isn't it? And that, my dear friends, is the heart of the secret I have uncovered." Finding the page he wanted, he dropped his voice conspiratorially low and continued. "Our ancestors used seven items that were all rich in magic: an enchanted flower that must be plucked at a certain time of day from a certain cliff, a magic herb that only grows in the wake of a lightning strike, a desert fruit that only ripens beneath the full moon, a pearl that formed in the saddest part of the sea, a heart-shaped rock buried in volcanic ash, a crystal hidden in a forgotten cave, and a piece of a fallen star." With one paw, he etched the path of a comet through the sky, and he conjured a lily at the end of it. Pollen shot out like a firework.

The fox sneezed as pollen landed on her nose, and candy sprayed around the room — her gift was to conjure candy, sometimes accidentally. There was a scramble to gather the candy. Charlie waited patiently for everyone to settle back down with their loot before he continued. But Holly kept her attention fixed on Charlie.

He held his notebook in the air. "Through my research, I have also learned the exact words to the spell that was cast on these items, the spell that created the magic water that changed the course of all our lives."

"Whoa!" Gus said.

"Brilliant!" Bluebell cried.

"But why?" Holly asked Charlie. She understood that it made a lovely story — it was nice to know more about their history — but that didn't explain why Charlie was making such a fuss. Or what any of this had to do with their new arrival.

He pressed the notebook to his heart. "Because I believe the spell must be recast. The magic water is failing, and that is the reason we are as we are. The Moon Mirror failed us when we drank from it."

That got everyone's attention. Startled, the porcupine rattled his quills. He scooted away from the skunk to avoid sticking her. Gawking at Charlie, the skunk didn't even notice the close call.

"You . . . you mean . . ." Leaf couldn't finish his sentence.

Grandly, Charlie said, "We weren't meant to have these powers! We were meant to have the kind of magic that true familiars have. Useful magic, that can be harnessed in many ways. It was a mistake that turned us into mistakes. And I aim to fix it."

"To fix *us*?" Holly asked. Like Leaf, she could barely say the words. It was an unimaginable idea.

"What do you mean?" Bluebell asked. "Do you suggest you

plan to change our destinies?" In a puff of pink, his hat transformed into a fedora. He tilted it at an angle between his ears, as if that made him look more dramatic.

"Indeed I do," Charlie said. "That is why I left — to determine how to reset our fates. And that is why I have returned — because I can't do it alone. I need a team to help me retrieve the seven magic ingredients and come with me to the top of Cloud Mountain, with the ingredients, to recast the spell."

All of them stared at Charlie.

And then they erupted into questions:

One of the shelterlings called out, "How do you know the Moon Mirror was broken?" Another asked, "How do you know it can be fixed?" A third asked, "Why do you need our help?"

Louder, the flamingo chimed in, "Yeah, how can we help? The wizards made it clear we're not good for much."

"And do we even want to help?" the toad asked. "Last time I went to the Moon Mirror on a fool's errand, I ended up here." He looked around quickly, "No offense."

"But, oh," the marmot said with a sigh, "to have real, useful magic! Wouldn't it be phenomenal?" Some of the animals began to argue among themselves, while others peppered Charlie with questions.

Holly tried to wrap her mind around what he was proposing. It was huge. Monumentally huge. It was impossible. Recast the spell? Fix the Moon Mirror? Fix *them*?

Zephyr zipped around the room. "How can the Moon Mirror be broken? Look at me! I'm fast! I have strength! I have endurance!

The water worked on me!" He smacked into Charlie's chair.

"Did it?" Leaf said. "It made you fast, but it left you with the reaction speed of a turtle."

Embarrassed, Zephyr pulled his head back into his shell. "I try."

"You crash," Leaf said. "All of us have broken magic."

Holly jumped in. "He's getting better!" Unlike Leaf, who never used his power on purpose, Zephyr practiced all the time. "Last week, he only knocked the kitchen table over twice."

"Clover has been practicing too," Gus added.

"As has Strawberry," Holly said. She'd been working with the skunk on extending the duration of her scents. After their last practice session, the barn had smelled like strawberries for a whole week. "Tangerine, show them what you've learned about extending your camouflage to things in your quills."

Demonstrating, Tangerine stuck a piece of candy onto his quills and shifted colors. The candy changed colors with him, blending in with his quills so that it was nearly invisible. But both he and the candy were bright orange against the blue carpet, not at all camouflaged.

As if they'd proved his point, Charlie said, "None of you would need to try so hard if the magic hadn't malfunctioned. Instead, we're stuck in between — neither ordinary nor familiars. That's why none of us can be truly happy. But we can fix that if we fix the Moon Mirror!"

Everyone chattered at once again, so loud it was hard to think.

From under the chair, in a loud, belligerent voice that cut through the rest, Periwinkle asked, "What does any of this have to do with me? I like my magic just fine as it is."

"You, my dear, are the key!" Charlie said. "I have determined the exact location of five of the ingredients — which will require volunteers to claim — but the final two . . . I will need you, sweet Periwinkle, and your special gift to help me find them." He waved in the air, and a bouquet of daisies appeared in his paw. Bending over, he laid the flowers next to the chair, where Periwinkle could see his gift. "Please, my dear. Will you help me? Will you help your fellow shelterlings?"

Holly peered under the chair at Periwinkle.

A paw darted out, grabbed the daisies, and then retreated beneath the chair. Sullenly, Periwinkle said, "Maybe I will, and maybe I won't. Not going to do it just 'cause you want me to. I make my own decisions."

Charlie blinked but recovered quickly. He conjured another flower bouquet, this time tulips and daffodils, and presented them to Holly. "If we work together, we can do this, but I will need several brave volunteers to help me. With seven items to find, I cannot do this alone. Help me, and I will fix you. You will not be mistakes anymore."

Fix me. Holly hadn't imagined that was possible. After all, she was just . . . an ordinary squirrel who had once had delusions of grandeur. She'd accepted that. She'd accepted the fact that she'd never be the next Savannah, who, with her wizard, had established a new home for a flock of winged ponies, or the next Quill, who, with his wizard, had saved hundreds of baby sea turtles by making them invisible until the tide turned. She wasn't going to go on any quests or have any adventures, unless you counted cleaning up the yard, harvesting tomatoes, or welcoming new arrivals.

Charlie kept talking, animatedly, describing exactly how to find each of the seven magic ingredients — east to the sea for the pearl, south toward the swamps for the herb . . . Holly couldn't focus on his words, though.

She was caught in a crystal-clear memory of the day she'd climbed Cloud Mountain: how excited she'd been as she followed the trail up to the peak and drank from the Moon Mirror. She remembered the ticklish tingle that had spread across her as the magic flowed through her body. She'd felt it in every bit of fur.

In that moment, she was certain that everything was going to become better. *She* would be better. She'd have a new purpose, a new place in the world. She'd be able to do important things, see other places, and make a difference in the lives of animals throughout the land. She was going to be a hero, working alongside her wizard, like the familiars of legend.

What if that dream *wasn't* over?

"Charlie," she asked, "is this really possible?"

"More than possible; it's necessary!" Charlie thumped his broad tail on the back of the chair for emphasis. "I have been patient for far too long — but now the time has come." Holly had never heard him sound so passionate. She marveled at this new Charlie. "We will right the wrong done to us!"

"All of us?" Pepper asked. "Me too?"

"Remind us all, my dear: What power did the Moon Mirror give you?"

"I'd rather not think about it," Pepper said.

Gently, Charlie said, "You can tell us."

The flamingo dropped her head down, her beak hanging between her long legs. "My left leg stretches," she mumbled.

Holly made a sympathetic chittering sound.

"Go ahead," Charlie said to Pepper. "Show us."

Pepper stood on one leg and concentrated. Her standing leg — and only that leg — stretched longer and longer. Tucked under her body, her other leg stayed short. She bumped into the ceiling and then shrank back down.

Encouraging as always, Gus said, "Look at how high you can get when you do that! You touched the ceiling! You should practice more."

"But I'm a bird. I don't need to become taller. I can fly." If she'd been human, Pepper's face would have been pink from embarrassment. As it was, she was already pink. "It's a useless power."

"Not as useless as mine has made me," Leaf said.

"You're not useless!" Zephyr said stoutly. "You're my friend!"

Bluebell said, "I did dream I would be more than a rabbit with hats." In a puff of pink, his hat transformed into a black pillbox hat with a mourning veil.

"I can move the entire universe two feet to the left," the garter snake, Dandelion, said. "That's a true power. But no one can tell, which is terribly disappointing." He coiled his body tightly and tucked his head within the coils. "I just wanted a power that can be recognized."

Others spoke up too: the bat who could only turn half invisible, the mouse who could turn all the way invisible but only when no one was watching, the duck who sparkled when she flapped, the toad who could make other animals yawn whenever he wanted (but why would he want to? he asked) . . .

Charlie nodded at all the shelterlings who had spoken. "We're failures. Each and every one of us. But we don't have to stay that way. We can change ourselves. It won't be easy, though. All my research agrees that in order for the spell to work, we need to place the seven ingredients at the edge of the Moon Mirror. It is absolutely essential we have all seven of them. Do you understand? If we don't have seven, we have nothing."

Holly nodded. She saw others around her looking solemn.

"And that is why I need help. I cannot do this alone. The items we need are in difficult-to-reach places, and retrieving them will require bravery, ingenuity, and strength of spirit."

All of them had that, Holly believed. It had required bravery to leave their homes and climb Cloud Mountain in the first place. If they could call on that again . . . "You're certain the spell will work?" she asked. "If we do this? If we can find all seven?"

"I've studied and researched it," he assured her. "If we go to Cloud Mountain with all the ingredients, my spell will work, and your lives will change. I promise that. You won't need to be shelterlings anymore."

She stared at him, and he waited for her, as patient as always. If she *didn't* try, how would she feel? He was offering them something that she'd never thought they'd have. A second chance to be a familiar, to be the kind of animal who could make a difference in the world. Wasn't that reason enough to try?

"Well, what do you say?" Charlie asked. "Are you ready for an adventure?"

Holly looked at her friends. Some looked uncertain, some anxious, but others looked hopeful, even excited.

"Yay, adventure!" Zephyr cried, and zipped across the living room. He crashed into a couch and spun around.

"We can't do it," Leaf objected, clinging to Zephyr's shell. "We aren't cut out for adventures. That's exactly what being a rejected familiar means! The wizards said we aren't good enough for quests. None of us. Not even you, Charlie."

True, the wizards had said that, in between laughing at her croissants and muffins. No matter how many bowls of parsnip soup she ate or how much she helped other shelterlings improve their powers, she was still just a little squirrel who wasn't made for adventures.

But what if *this* kind of adventure was different?

Gus leaned over and said, "Well, Holly? What do you think?"

She looked at Charlie, on his favorite chair, waiting for volunteers to help him change all their lives. She looked at the other shelterlings, all together in one room. "I think we have to try." Holly drew herself up, with her tail fluffed behind her. "Charlie, I'd like to volunteer."

CHAPTER FIVE

By nightfall, Charlie had all his volunteers, and Holly was having second thoughts.

She'd tried adventuring once, when she'd climbed Cloud Mountain to drink from the Moon Mirror, and it had gone poorly. She wasn't cut out for quests or heroics. Squirrels usually weren't. There was a reason that most familiars were cats, owls, wolves, or other animals who didn't scamper up trees to hide at the first sign of danger.

Except that she *would* like to see someplace new.

A cliff with a magic flower, for instance.

Holly looked up at the sky from the front porch. It was dusk, and the first few stars were poking through. The crickets had begun their song out in the fields, and she saw the shadow of a bat, swooping through the air to scoop up a delicious dinner of insects. Absently, she conjured up a muffin and nibbled on it.

Holly the Adventurer. It had a nice ring to it.

Behind her, she heard the familiar rustle of soft feathers. Gus glided across the porch to settle on the bench. He folded his wings. "Nice night," he said.

Sharing the muffin with Gus, Holly climbed onto the oversize nest and sat in the center of one of the pillows. "It is." She could hear the chatter from inside. With so many creatures talking at once, the words blurred into one another. They sounded like crickets chirping at different pitches.

"I know what you're thinking," Gus said, after he'd swallowed his half of the muffin.

"You do?" Holly asked. She hadn't thought she was so easy to read. As Charlie had distributed the various quests, she didn't think anyone could tell she'd been imagining herself as the next Calla, working with her wizard to create a growth spell to build a bridge that united two islands. It wasn't a thing that squirrels generally dreamed of doing.

Or at least that was what her neighbor in her old forest had told her, when she'd announced she was going to Cloud Mountain: *Holly, really, now, that's not a thing a squirrel does! Traipsing off after magic! Mixing with strange animals! Stay in your forest. Tend to your acorns. Winter will be coming soon enough, and you should be here, preparing, hiding your hoard and defending your territory. You go wandering off . . . well, there's just no telling what will happen.*

She'd been right about that.

"You're thinking about who ate the rest of the strawberries," Gus said.

"Yes. That's it. Exactly what I was thinking." She wondered if Gus would want to come on a quest with her. She really couldn't imagine adventuring on her own. But she wasn't quite sure how to ask.

"It couldn't have been Periwinkle," Gus said. "She's still avoiding talking to Charlie. Or anyone, really. She's holed up in her ribbon room again. Ooh, maybe we could set a trap. Paint rocks to look like strawberries."

"That's a terrible idea," Holly said. "Someone could eat them and get sick. Also a terrible idea: coming with me on a quest to find the magic flower. But will you do it anyway?"

"Huh?"

It was not a resounding yes. She considered pretending she'd said something completely different. Wrapping her tail around her belly, she plucked at a tuft of fur. "It's a silly idea. Never mind. I don't even remember which way Charlie said to go."

"Five miles southwest, then follow the river to the Gray Hills. Go into the Crescent Forest until you reach the cliffs. When the sun hits the crack in the cliff, that's when you have to pick the flower. It only grows in one place in the world, and it has to be picked at a specific time on a day when the sun shines right on the blossom. Can't be any other flower. I, uh, memorized it when Charlie said it. Just in case."

"Gus, you're amazing!" Holly said.

Gus flew toward the door. "I'll tell the others we're both going so they can cheer us on!"

Scurrying ahead of him, Holly blocked the door — or at least a small portion of the bottom of the doorway. Tiny paws out, she said, "Wait, maybe don't?"

He fluttered to land on the porch. "Why not?"

"I just don't want all the fuss, that's all. It's not . . . I'm not . . ."

"Are you afraid we're going to fail? Is that it?"

She nodded.

"Holly, you can't start an adventure expecting failure," Gus said. "Everyone knows that. You have to start with full confidence and possibly a parade —"

Bluebell leaped over Holly's head and landed on the nest with the pink pillows. The twigs crackled beneath him, but the rabbit stood on his hind legs, posed with one arm raised, and said, "Indeed, dear friends, the owl speaks the truth! Be certain of your purpose, resolute of spirit, and proud of your flatulence!"

Both Holly and Gus stared at him.

"I'm not sure that last one was quite what you meant to say," Holly said.

"Oh, I meant every word."

Holly decided she didn't want to know any more details. "Bluebell, Gus and I are heading out to find the flower. If you could let the others know —"

Bluebell leaped from the nest onto the porch railing. "I will sing it from the rooftops. Brave Holly and brave Asparagus, embarking on their very first adventure together! It is the evolution of a beautiful friendship, founded on mutual respect and admiration. Together, they will achieve greatness."

Holly finished her request: "If you could let the others know *after* we leave?"

He transformed his headwear into a floppy, wide-brimmed hat with an ostrich feather that drooped over his eyes. He blew the feather backwards. "If that's what you wish, then I shall witness your departure and your grand return and report it to the others, like a bard of old!"

"Thank you, Bluebell," Holly said. "You'll be an excellent bard." She wasn't sure what a bard was, but if it made him happy, that was good.

He struck a pose. "I shall begin with a song."

Gus leaned closer to Holly. "I think that's our cue to leave. *Before* he starts singing."

Holly hadn't really planned on leaving instantly, but there wasn't much point in dithering. Gus was right — she'd heard Bluebell sing before, and she didn't need to hear it again. He had very little regard for pitch.

And so they began their quest, right then and there, as simply as that, with Holly walking and Gus flying along the path to the trellis, away from the Shelter for Rejected Familiars and out into the great wide world.

✦

Five miles southwest, Gus had said. That was the first direction.

I can do that, Holly thought. Average range for a squirrel was five miles. She could travel that in a day — or a night, in this case — and then, after a rest, they'd tackle the next leg of the journey. She guessed the cliffs were about five or six days away at squirrel speed. Of course, it would be nice to cross the distance a little quicker, but one could only scurry fast for so long. Besides, it was a nice night for a stroll. As it grew darker, the sky boasted more stars, and she loved to admire them in all their splendor. Humming to herself, she kept her eyes on the sky as she trotted across the field.

"Um, Holly?"

"Yes, Gus?"

"Are we really going to travel at this speed the whole time?" he asked.

She swished her tail at him. "This is a perfectly reasonable speed. If I run full tilt, I'll be exhausted too quickly. It's smarter to conserve energy." She sniffed at a flower as they passed. In the moonlight, it was as blue-gray as everything else, but it still smelled sweet.

"Yes, but wouldn't flying be faster?"

Holly laughed. "I'm not a flying squirrel." She knew he always thought the best of her, but really. "Gray squirrels leap from branch to branch, but unfortunately, we aren't in a forest."

"You could fly on wings."

"I'm not likely to sprout wings."

Landing, he waddled beside her. Owls have an awkward gait that made him sway side to side as if he were about to topple over. "I meant you could fly on *my* wings. You could climb on my back and ride on me. If we fly, we could reach the cliffs in half the time."

Holly halted and stared at him. She couldn't tell if he was being serious. That was . . . She'd never heard of such a thing. "You'd look ridiculous with a squirrel on your back."

"Why should I care about that?" he asked.

"I . . ." She supposed he shouldn't care.

He lowered himself, then held still as she scrambled onto his back. She sank into his plush feathers and grasped the roots of a handful of them. Squirrels didn't fly on owls, of course, and she spared a moment to contemplate what her neighbor would say about this. *She'd probably faint at the very thought of it,* Holly thought. She imagined flying past her old trees just to witness that reaction.

Gus bent his knees, and she felt his muscles tense beneath her. He stretched out his wings, and then, with a powerful but silent flap, he launched into the air. Holly felt wind rush against her face, and she held on tight.

With every flap, he rose higher, and the flower fields dropped away beneath them. Holly peered over his shoulder and saw the ground below them shrink into shadows. She looked forward and saw the horizon with the last glow leftover from sunset.

The moon was already bright, nearly full.

She supposed this was more practical. Owls could see better in the dark than squirrels — he was nocturnal by nature. She wasn't meant to be out wandering through fields in the night.

A more practical option, yes, she thought.

And a more amazing one.

Holly had never supposed she would love flying. She was meant to be a paws-on-the-ground, head-in-the-trees kind of rodent. But the air up here tasted as sweetly clear as a stream after the snow melted, and the song of the wind filled her ears. She closed her eyes, listening to it and to the very soft, near-silent whoosh of Gus's rare wing beats. He could glide a long time on outspread wings, and it made their flight feel even more wondrous.

When she opened her eyes, the moon shone in front of them, bright and glorious. It bathed the fields below in a gentle gray. "It's beautiful," she said.

"I've been wanting to show you this."

"Show me what?"

"The world." He tilted, and they soared toward what looked like a black ribbon, the kind that Periwinkle had used to decorate her room. A river, she realized. She remembered that the directions said to follow a river.

"If I were you, I'd never stop flying," Holly said.

"Watch this," Gus said, and he dived down.

Skimming over the surface of the river, he touched the water with his wing tips. She felt spray in her face and laughed in delight. Holding on tight with her hind legs, Holly let go of his feathers and spread her front paws wide to feel the full wind and river spray.

For two days, they followed the river to the Gray Hills and then aimed for the Crescent Forest. By the time dawn sneaked over the eastern horizon and spilled its light across the land on the third day, Holly and Gus could see the cliffs, rising up out of the trees.

"Charlie said that when the sun hits the cliffs, that's when we pluck the flower," Gus called. "We should have a little time to rest before the sun is in the right position. It has to be the flower that grows in a crack on the cliff, and it has to be the moment the angle of the sun hits the open petals. According to Charlie's research, there's only one spot where the cliff isn't too sheer for the flower to grow. It should be easy to spot, but we have to get the timing exactly right."

"Great!" Holly said. "Let's get as close as we can so we're ready — what is *that*?"

Ahead of them, stretched across the cliffs, was a shimmering web. It looked like a spiderweb, except for its golden glow. In the center, caught in the strands, was a cat.

CHAPTER SIX

Holly held tight to Gus's feathers as he flew closer to the golden web. She'd never seen anything like it: it looked like wisps of sun had been woven together. The strands sparkled in the early light, flashing like thousands of tiny jewels as they twisted in the wind.

The cat, suspended in the center, called to them, "Hey! Hello there! Over here!"

"Are you all right?" Holly called to the cat.

"Sure, just hanging out," he said. "Enjoying the breeze."

Okay, it was a curious choice, but she didn't want to criticize another animal, especially one she didn't know. "Glad to hear it," Holly said politely. "We're looking for —"

The cat cut her off. "Of course I'm not all right! Do I look like I'm all right?" He tried to swat with his paw, but the webbing held him tight. "I'm stuck! Please, help me get free! Argh!" As he squirmed, he got himself even more tied up in the strands.

Gus flew closer.

"Not too close!" the cat shouted. "You'll get caught too!"

Gus veered away from the golden web. Flying near but not too near, the owl rose and fell with the wind that swirled around the cliffs.

The strands stretched from rock to rock, crisscrossing in an interwoven pattern, blocking the cliff. The web was thickest over a triangular crack in the stone. It was the only break in the sheer rock face of the cliff that she could see. And it was completely inaccessible. She wondered if that was where the magic flower was growing. She guessed it was.

"How can we help?" Holly asked the cat.

"Normally, my wizard would —"

Gus flapped excitedly. "You're a familiar?"

"Yes, and my wizard —"

"We have magic too!" Gus said.

Holly winced. Now the cat was going to think —

"This is fantastic!" the cat said. "I'm saved! Get your wizards and spell me out of here!"

Still holding on to Gus's feathers, she wrapped her tail around her and hid behind the fluff. She did *not* want to explain she could only conjure pastries. It was one thing to admit that to Periwinkle, but to tell an actual familiar . . . The cat was waiting for a response.

"Oh, we don't have wizards," Gus said cheerfully. "They didn't want us. We're shelterlings."

Sighing, the cat sagged against the strands. "I should have known it was too good to be true. I'm doomed. And my poor wizard—she's down in the forest, caught in a sleep spell. Without me, she'll sleep forever. And without her, I'll be stuck forever."

"That's horrible!" Gus said.

"If she'd just listened to me, like a true partner would —" He cut himself off. "Never mind."

"You must have been on a very exciting quest to have been caught in a web and have your wizard trapped in a spell," Gus said. "We're on a quest for a magic flower. Unfortunately, I think it might be growing behind your web."

"Inside the dragon's cave? Ha! Good luck with that," the cat said.

"The . . . what?" Holly squeaked.

She gawked at the cliff in horror. She'd thought the crack was a ledge, not a cave, and it was supposed to hold a flower, not a dragon.

"We were hired by the townsfolk to rid them of the dragon who lives in these cliffs," the cat said. "They discovered the dragon roaming the forest near where they were building new homes, and we were sent to vanquish it. Yay. If I never have to face another — Anyway, what no one told us was that this dragon can work magic. It caught my wizard in a sleep spell before we could speak a single spell of our own, and then, when I tried to escape, it cast this web spell and trapped me."

An actual dragon lived here?

A spell-casting dragon who could trap both a wizard and a familiar?

This was more adventure than Holly had bargained for. She'd loved the journey here — flight was amazing and wonderful and all the superlative words she could think of — but this was too much. She wasn't ready for this. It required a proper hero, a familiar like Calla or Quill, not a squirrel who could only conjure pastries. Croissants couldn't defeat a dragon. "Can't you use your own magic to free yourself?"

"Obviously not. Don't you know the downside to being a familiar? It's one of those fun details that everyone glosses over until it's too late. A familiar is tied to their wizard. Our bond makes it possible for us to cast the highest-level spells, but I can't work any magic without her, except my own personal kind, which isn't so useful in this situation."

"What can you do?" Holly asked. It had to be more useful than pastries.

He closed his eyes and concentrated. A second later he opened his eyes, and two beams of light blazed out and across the forest. "Generate light. During my test to become a familiar, I had to navigate a maze in the dark. Once my wizard saw that, she knew she'd have a use for me. My power has enabled her to accept nighttime quests, but it's not much help now." He blinked, and the light vanished. "And now that she's gotten herself stuck under a sleep spell in the forest . . . It's humiliating to be this helpless. But I suppose you wouldn't understand that."

Holly knew all about being humiliated, and it wasn't anything she'd wish on another creature. "I do understand."

The cat let out a plaintive yowl, like an off-key song. "My wizard and I are supposed to be heroes! That's what I was promised when I bonded with her. We were supposed to go on adventures together, taking on quests to protect the land from whatever threatened it. Instead, look at us! We're pathetic!" He yowled louder, and below, birds took flight, cawing to one another.

Holly knew what that was like too, to feel disappointment. "We'll find you a wizard and familiar who aren't caught in a spell, they'll can come and rescue you, and you'll be back to adventuring in no time."

"There are no wizards nearby for miles," the cat said. "That's why the village hired us. We were the only ones close enough to answer their call. By the time you find anyone with the skill to unravel these spells, the dragon will have returned to finish me off!"

"Oh my," Holly said. "I'm sure the dragon won't actually *eat* you. That would be rude."

Glumly, the cat said, "He said he'd always wanted to try cat."

Or maybe the dragon *would* eat him. You could never tell with unknown carnivores — they might see you as a friend, or they might see you as lunch. Holly poked her nose over Gus's shoulder to look down at the forest below. She hoped dragons weren't interested in the taste of squirrel or owl.

Regardless, they certainly couldn't allow the cat to become a dragon's latest taste treat. The poor creature looked miserable. His whiskers drooped, and his tail dangled between the strands. There had to be a way to help. Holly whispered to Gus, "We can't just leave him like this."

Still flapping, Gus did another swooping pass by the cat. "I know. I've met you. You can't stand it when any animal is unhappy. You always try to help. That's one of the things I like best about you, Holly. So what's our plan?"

Holly called to the cat, "How strong is the web?"

"Strong enough to hold me." Demonstrating, the cat squirmed.

As he twisted and flailed, Holly saw the strands that were anchored to the rocks strain. If the cat were stronger . . . or heavier . . . *Oh dear.* She had an idea, but it was likely to be terrifying and dangerous, and she should probably just forget she'd ever had it.

"You know what to do," Gus said. It wasn't even a question. Just a statement.

"What makes you say that?" she asked him.

"You always know what to do," he said with confidence. "You always fix everything."

"Sure, if you mean cleaning up parsnip soup or repairing a porch roof," Holly said. "Not rescuing a familiar from a dragon's trap! It's not in my skill set."

"But you have an idea how to do it," Gus said. "Admit it."

"I . . . do."

"Am I going to like it?" Gus asked.

I'm going to hate it, she thought. But Gus . . . "You're going to love it." And before she could talk herself out of it, she told him her idea: "Remember the day we met, your arrival day? How you broke the roof of the porch?"

"Sure. I got so excited that I flew up high and . . . oh. You want me to do *that?*"

The cat called, "What are you two whispering about?" He twisted, and the golden webbing shifted with him. Every time he moved, he cocooned himself tighter.

Holly called to him, "Just stay where you are, okay?"

"Ha! Very funny," the cat said. "Never met a squirrel with a sense of humor before."

She tightened her grip on the owl's feathers. "Fly, Gus. Fly high."

Gus flapped his wings hard, and air whooshed behind him. "Woo-hoo!" he called, with the joy of someone who has just been asked to do the very thing he's always dreamed of doing. Holly tried not to look down as he climbed higher and higher.

Above, the clouds looked as if they were touchable. She felt the sun warming her fur, and the wind rushing around them. After a few minutes, she peeked down — the cliffs were below them, and the cat was a speck within an array of sparkles.

This is a really bad idea, Holly thought.

But it might work.

"Do it!" she called to Gus. She buried her paws as deep into his feathers as she could. "Now!"

Tucking his wings against his body, he solidified beneath her. She felt the feathers transform around her paws, hardening into granite that held her snugly, and as he shifted, he plummeted.

She screamed and felt as if the air were being ripped from her throat. Her stomach was left behind in the clouds, and her skin and fur fluttered over her bones. Securely anchored to the stone owl, she fell and fell, hurtling toward the web.

She saw the glittering mesh rising toward them, and she caught a glimpse of the cat's face, horrified, as they slammed into the webbing.

It tore away from the cliff.

Yes! she thought.

And then she looked down again.

The forest was coming fast. "Gus, you did it! Change back!"

He didn't answer. She swatted his stone back with her tail. "Gus! Gus!"

The trees rushed toward her, the tops of the pine trees like spears. She screamed again and heard the cat screaming too — he was falling as well, within the webbing.

"Gus!"

His stone body softened. She felt feathers beneath her. Stretching out his wings, he glided over the tops of the trees. She heard the leaves rustle as his stomach brushed against the canopy. He landed on a branch.

The golden webbing drifted down around them like a shimmering snowfall.

"Ahhh!" The cat fell beside them, and then the web caught on the branches. His fall abruptly stopped. He dangled, cocooned in the web, from the tree. He stopped screaming.

Holly called to him, "Are you all right?"

In a stunned and amazed voice, the cat said, "Yes. I actually am. You saved me."

CHAPTER SEVEN

"My name is Saffron," the cat said.

"I'm Holly," Holly said politely, "and this is Gus." With her paws and teeth, she tore at the webbing that was wrapped around Saffron. Once his claws were free, he began to cut through the strands himself. That went faster.

"Thank you for rescuing me," he said, spitting out the webbing. "That was . . . an unusual technique. But it worked. How can I repay you? Without my wizard, I can't do much, but I'll do what I can. You said you were looking for a magic flower?"

Gus nodded. "Yes, it's supposed to grow in a crack in the cliff. Guess that's the one — the dragon's cave. I don't see any other possibilities." He squinted up at the sky, and so did Holly. The sun was far higher than it had been when they'd reached the cliffs. The yellow light was already creeping across the rock.

"How about a different flower?" Saffron asked. "There are lots of nice ones in the forest. Or you could try a garden in town."

"Sorry, but that's the only one that will work," Gus said. "And we have to pick it when the sun touches its petals, which will be . . . in a little while. We should have plenty of time."

The cat bit through more strands and then spat them out. "Yeah, see, about that cave? That's where the dragon keeps his hoard. If you go near it, he'll think you're trying to steal from him."

"I would never steal," Holly said primly.

Saffron snorted. "You can try explaining that to the dragon."

"Perhaps I should."

"Ha. The only way you'll be able to reach that flower is if my wizard and I defeat the dragon," Saffron said, "and the only way *that* will happen is if I rescue my wizard."

Well then, the solution seemed simple. "Okay, so we'll help you rescue your wizard." After all, they'd successfully saved the cat. How much harder could it be to wake a wizard? Of course, there was a dragon involved . . .

The cat seemed surprised. "You will?"

Glancing at Gus to make sure he agreed with her, Holly said, "Of course we will." They'd already come this far. Besides, it was the right thing to do, though she wasn't sure exactly how she and Gus could help against a dragon. Dragons were rumored to be quite large, fire-breathing, and foul-tempered. She'd never actually met one before. *I like helping creatures*, she reminded herself. *And Saffron needs help.*

"You know, I always thought rejected familiars were . . ." Saffron trailed off, as if he couldn't think of an adjective that wasn't insulting.

Holly appreciated that he didn't finish that sentence.

"Do rejected familiars often go on their own quests?" Saffron asked instead.

"This is our first," Gus said proudly.

Saffron shook his head in amazement. "Wow. I'm very glad your first quest took you this way. I don't know how long I would have been stuck there if you hadn't come along."

Our first quest. Holly liked those words. She wondered if Flint, the familiar who, with his wizard, had levitated a train to save a lizard who was about to be flattened, would have called this a quest. Maybe he would have.

"Happy to help," Holly said to Saffron. "Where is your wizard? And the dragon?"

"Follow me!" He bounded into the underbrush.

She scampered up the trunk of a tree into the branches. It felt delightful to be back in a forest again. As the cat padded through the ferns, vines, and bushes, Holly ran along the branches, leaping from tree to tree. It was nearly as good as flying. She thought she should visit forests more often. The shelter's orchard just wasn't the same as a forest that was thick with so many trees that the branches blocked the sky. Gus flew between the trees, weaving around the trunks.

This forest didn't feel so different from her old home. It had the same mix of oaks, maples, birches, and pines. She recognized blueberry and blackberry bushes, as well as the lily of the valley that grew in the shade near them. The smells were the same — earthy and pine-scented, heavy with the rich tang of old leaves — and so were the sounds of birds calling to one another from distant perches.

She would've thought that a forest with a dragon in it would feel different. More ominous. But the birds still sang, the flowers still bloomed, and the breeze still blew through thick, lush leaves.

Maybe no one told them there's a dragon here, Holly thought.

Or maybe the dragon was nicer than Saffron had implied. Of course, the dragon had captured both the cat and his wizard, plus threatened to eat Saffron, which was beyond rude, though not unexpected for a carnivore in the wild.

She really hoped the familiar had a plan for rescuing his wizard.

Dropping down onto his belly, the cat crawled through the grass. Holly took that as her cue to move more carefully, disturbing as few leaves as possible. Her nose twitched as she smelled some other squirrel's nut stash, but she left it alone.

In a few minutes, they came upon a clearing. And in the center of the clearing lay the dragon, curled up like a cat. A very, very large cat.

Holly had known the dragon would be big. What she hadn't grasped was precisely *how* big. To say he was the size of a house would not have been an exaggeration. The ridges on his scaly back were even with the tops of the trees. His thick tail was wrapped around his body and sported spikes that were as tall as Holly. His mouth was so full of teeth that several fangs stuck out beyond his lips. Smoke drifted up from his nostrils.

Okay, now I've seen a dragon, she thought. *Maybe we should go?* She didn't know what she'd been thinking, volunteering to help.

This wasn't a task for a little squirrel. She'd gotten caught up in the excitement of rescuing Saffron from the web. Holly cleared her throat to suggest they reconsider —

But the cat was creeping closer.

She saw where Saffron was aiming: the prone body of a female human wearing wizard robes, lying beside the dragon's right forepaw. Her wizard staff was nestled next to her, like a teddy bear alongside a slumbering child.

Both the wizard and the dragon were asleep.

"Well, we said we wanted an adventure," Gus whispered as he landed softly behind her. He barely rustled the leaves as he perched. She was glad owls were naturally quiet.

"We should have discussed a plan," Holly whispered back.

"I think the plan is he rescues his wizard. We're backup, in case something goes —"

As Saffron reached the wizard's side, the dragon's eyes popped open. His pupils were vertical like a snake's, but much, much larger than any snake eyes that Holly had ever seen, and his irises were golden green. He exhaled, and a wave of heat rolled across the clearing.

"— wrong," Gus finished. "Get down!"

Holly scampered down the tree trunk, while Gus plummeted from the branches. The dragon roared, and flames poured out of his mouth, high above the sleeping wizard. They licked at the trees, and the dead leaves caught fire. On the forest floor, Holly and Gus blew at the sparks and stomped on them.

The cat Saffron leaped on top of his wizard. "You do not frighten me, dragon!"

"Watch out!" Gus yelled as the dragon inhaled to breathe fire again.

Saffron yelped and dived into the bushes.

This is absurd, Holly thought. Countless birds, rodents, insects, and other animals lived in this forest and relied on it not being burned. She scurried through the blackberry bushes to circle around the clearing so that she had a better view of the dragon.

Any creature smart enough to do spells like creating the golden web and causing a wizard to sleep had to be smart enough to reason with, she thought. As the dragon reared back to aim at the spot where Saffron was hiding, Holly said loudly and sharply from within the bushes, "Stop! You're going to burn the trees!"

Just about to exhale, the dragon halted. "Excuse me?" Sparks spurted out with his words and fizzled in the air.

Saffron hissed. "What are you doing? You can't talk to it!"

The dragon heard him, swung his head in the direction of the cat's voice, and breathed flames. Saffron yelped again and ran up a tree. The dragon inhaled deeply, preparing to breathe fire at the branches.

Before he could exhale, Holly said loudly, "I said, stop it!"

Smoke curled out of the dragon's nostrils. "No one tells me what to do or not do."

"Well, maybe someone should," Holly said, "because you're behaving very badly." She curled her tail over her mouth, unable to believe she'd just said that, *and* in the same kind of tone the older squirrels in the forest used with their kits — or like she herself used when Zephyr crashed into one table too many or Strawberry got carried away with changing odors. But she kept going. "Lots of animals rely on this forest. It's their home. You can't burn it down."

Sticking his neck out, the dragon peered into the foliage. "You aren't the wizard's familiar who was invading my home earlier. Who are you? Are you another wizard's familiar?"

"I'm not," Holly said.

The nearby ferns withered under the dragon's breath, and Holly began to shake. She wished she'd kept quiet.

"Who are you to think you can speak to me? Do you not know what I am? Have you not heard the tales?" He posed in profile, his jaws open to display his many, many sharp teeth. "They say I am fire. They say I am fear. They say I am the terror that lurks in the hearts of man."

"I . . . I'm not a man," Holly said. "Or a familiar. I'm just a squirrel."

"'Just-a-squirrels' don't speak to me," the dragon said. "I ask again, and I demand you answer: What are you? Show yourself."

She wanted to bolt in the opposite direction. Every instinct inside her screamed to flee up a tree and hide in the branches. But doing so wouldn't help Saffron and his wizard — or the creatures who needed the forest to remain unburned.

I will help them, Holly thought.

She had to get the dragon to listen to her, and the first step in making that happen was to gain his trust. Like she was working on with Periwinkle. Except the dragon was a *lot* less friendly. And had a *lot* more teeth. Taking a deep breath, she stepped out of the blackberry bushes.

Hidden, Saffron hissed at her. "What are you doing? That's a *dragon!*"

Before the dragon could breathe fire at the cat again, Holly said, "I'm down here."

Inhaling, the dragon swung his head toward her — and then, seeing her, he stopped. "You *are* a squirrel. Or you look like one. You could be a wizard in disguise."

"Why would a wizard disguise herself as a squirrel?"

"To talk to me," the dragon said. "To trick me."

From the trees Gus called, "You just said that squirrels don't talk to you."

The dragon let out a blast of fire toward his voice, but Gus was already airborne, gliding silently to another tree. The flames singed the pine needles. They curled up and fell like rain on the forest floor. Holly breathed a sigh of relief as Gus landed safely on a pine tree out of the dragon's line of sight.

"No wizard would change into an ordinary squirrel," Holly said to the dragon. "And why would they want to trick you, anyway?"

"Everyone knows humans want to trick dragons. They want to steal our hoards!" The dragon stomped on the ground, and the forest floor shook. The ferns quivered, and a few leaves fell off nearby trees.

"No, they don't," Holly said.

"Ha. You *must* be a squirrel. You don't know what you're speaking of. Humans are thieves!"

She asked Saffron, "Are they? Do they want to steal the dragon's hoard?"

"Absolutely not," Saffron said from the top branches of an oak tree. "We wouldn't have taken the quest if they'd provoked the dragon. Told them as much. What they *want* is for him to stop terrorizing their town."

The dragon raised himself up onto his hind legs. He was larger than the trees; his head was well above the canopy. She had to tilt her own head back to see all of the vast creature.

"I do not terrorize," the dragon declared.

Holly wanted to bolt through the forest, but she didn't know if she could outrun the dragon's flames. She was already too exposed. She had to trust that he would listen to reason. "You said yourself that you're the terror in the hearts of man."

"I am terrifying, but I do not terrorize," the dragon said. Privately, Holly thought that was a very fine line. "I cannot control how others see me. I do nothing to them, yet they persist in being frightened of me. They see my teeth and assume I will bite. They see my fire and assume they will burn."

"Kind of a logical assumption when you keep trying to cook me," Saffron muttered from his tree. Gus hushed him.

Holly considered what to say next. In a way, the dragon reminded her of Periwinkle, complaining that others called her a thief after she'd found — and kept — their lost items. "You can't change how they've seen you in the past, but you can change how they see you in the future. Breathing fire at anyone who approaches you is not the way to make friends."

The dragon puffed out smoke. "I do not want to 'make friends.' I am a rare and magnificent dragon. I need no one."

Everyone needed friends, Holly thought. Especially rare and magnificent dragons who had probably never had any. "Then what do you want?"

"To be left alone," he said promptly.

"So you never went near the town?" Holly asked. "Never breathed fire on it?" She was trying to understand what had upset the townspeople so much. Aside from the teeth. And the claws. And the sheer massive size.

The dragon huffed a tiny tendril of smoke. "I did burn one of their structures — an unfinished barn clearly designed to hold stolen treasure — as a warning to thieves to stay away."

Ah, that explained it.

"It could have been designed to hold cows," Gus pointed out. "Did you ask?"

"Of course I didn't ask," the dragon said. "You cannot ask a human anything. They start screaming and running around. Sometimes they throw rocks. Horrible creatures. Everyone knows that humans are irrational."

She was beginning to understand. "You saw the humans building what you thought was a treasure vault, and you decided they were thieves. The humans saw a dragon burning their building, and they decided you were a threat to their town. But you never actually talked to each other."

"They started it. Thieves. Vandals! They chopped down trees in *my* forest and started building their homes on *my* home."

Gus asked, "Did they know you lived here?"

"I do not know what humans know or don't know," the dragon said.

From his perch in the oak, Saffron said, "They didn't know."

Immediately, the dragon blasted fire in his direction.

Oh, for goodness' sake. "Enough with the fire! There's a straight-forward solution to all of this, if you'll just listen instead of lashing out." Holly waved her tail from side to side for emphasis. "Now, will you listen to me?"

"I don't even know you. You could be thieves too."

"My name is Holly, and my friends are Gus and Saffron. We aren't interested in your hoard. Gus and I are here for a magic flower that grows on the cliff, and Saffron is here with his wizard to mediate a truce between you and the townspeople."

Saffron said, "That's not why —"

Gus shushed him.

"You want a truce, don't you?" Holly asked the dragon. "You want the townspeople to leave you alone? And the townspeople want to build their town in peace."

"In *my* forest," the dragon grumbled.

"All we have to do, then, is find a way for all of you to have what you want."

Saffron spoke up. "The humans could pay you for use of your land. Humans do that sort of thing with other humans all the time."

This time the dragon didn't try to breathe fire on the cat. "Excuse me?"

Holly thought that was an excellent idea. "Yes! The townspeople could contribute to your hoard, and in exchange, you let them build their buildings in peace."

"They were happy enough to pay a wizard to keep you away," Gus said. "I'm sure they'd be happy to pay you directly for the same thing."

"My wizard and I can negotiate on your behalf," Saffron offered, "if you'll let her wake."

Settling his wings on his back, the dragon appeared to be considering it. Really, it was the most sensible solution, Holly thought. All of this was based on a misunderstanding. If they'd just *talk* to each other . . . "You could talk at a safe distance at first," Holly said. "You don't have to let them in your forest until you want to."

"I never want to."

"You share it with birds and squirrels." Even after the dragon's fiery display, she could hear birds chirping in the distance.

"Birds don't cut down my trees. And squirrels don't send wizards and familiars with spells to try to drive me out of my home." The dragon looked at her with its enormous snakelike eyes. "Squirrels normally don't even speak to me."

"People don't *have* to cut down trees or send wizards," Holly said. "That's why you talk with them. Without fire. You negotiate and find a compromise. Or you at least try. If it works, your hoard will grow. But if you just use fire, they're going to keep coming back with more ways — and more wizards and familiars — to try to force you out."

"And if they refuse to listen?"

"You haven't even given them a chance."

Smoke curled from the dragon's nostrils as he considered some more.

"Let them prove they can be different than you think they are," Holly pleaded. "You might be surprised."

The dragon lowered his head so that his eye was even with her. She saw her reflection mirrored in his vast snakelike iris. "You truly believe this will work?"

"I do," she said firmly. "I believe that if you try, you and the humans can find an arrangement that makes you happy and the townspeople happy."

He swung his neck to look at Saffron. "If I do this thing and speak with the humans . . . no wizard or familiar will ever bother me again?"

"If you wake my wizard, she can tell the other wizards to stay out of it," Saffron said. "But you need to wake her."

"I do not trust wizards," the dragon said with another huff of smoke.

Holly jumped in. "Saffron will promise not to work any spells with her against you. Won't you, Saffron?"

"I promise," the cat said.

"Isn't it at least worth a try?" she asked the dragon.

Thinking, the dragon kneaded the pine-needle-covered forest floor with one paw. Holly waited, trying to be as patient as Charlie. At last, he said, "That would be acceptable."

"Yay!" Holly said. She ran in an excited circle.

The dragon bent his head toward the sleeping wizard, nudged her with the tip of his nose, and recited a string of syllables that sounded like a spell. The wizard began to stir. Saffron hurried to her side.

"Thank you," Saffron said to the dragon as his wizard yawned and stretched.

From his tree, Gus piped up, "One more thing? If you don't mind, could we enter the mouth of your cave to pick a flower? The sun is minutes away from being in the right position, and the flower is supposed to be growing just inside your home."

A growl began deep in the dragon's throat. "My hoard —"

Holly jumped in quickly. "We promise we won't touch your hoard. I'm a squirrel — my idea of treasure is acorns." It was an easy promise to both make and keep.

"Only the flower," the dragon said.

"Only the flower," Holly repeated.

"Woo-hoo!" Gus said. He flew down to Holly, and she climbed onto his back. "Hurry, the sun is almost there. If we're quick enough, we can still pick it today!"

She waved at the dragon and called, "Thank you! And good luck!"

"Thank you!" Saffron called to them. "A million times thank

you! If you ever need anything, don't hesitate to ask! You have my friendship!"

"And you have ours!" Holly called back.

The dragon and the cat, together with the confused-but-awake wizard, watched them fly up out of the forest toward the cliff, as the sun inched closer to the crack in the rocks, the dragon's cave. As sunlight touched the inside, Holly saw the flower.

Warmed by the sun, its petals peeled open. It glowed like a star.

"Quickly, Holly!" Gus urged.

Holly scrambled off his back and onto the cliff. She hurried just inside the opening of the cave and saw the sparkle of heaps of gold and jewels. Ignoring all the treasure, she cupped her paws around the magic blossom. Swiftly, before the light moved on, she plucked it.

It kept glowing.

We did it, she thought.

She held it gently in her front paws as she climbed onto Gus's back. He glided away from the cliffs, the dragon, and the forest, flying toward home.

CHAPTER EIGHT

Cradling the magic flower in her front paws, Holly slid off of Gus's back onto the lawn of the Shelter for Rejected Familiars. After so much time flying, her hind legs wobbled a little.

"Air legs," Gus told her. "You'll feel steady in a minute or two."

"Guess I'm a flying squirrel after all," Holly said. "Who knew?"

Gus laughed, and so did Holly. She felt giddy. They'd done it! She wanted to run to the roof and dance. Or to jump back on Gus and fly again.

Bluebell hopped out of the house onto the porch. "Huzzah! More adventurers have returned!" he proclaimed. He transformed his hat into a celebratory bonnet festooned with pom-poms. "I must know: Were you victorious?"

"Yes!" Gus said, with a hoot for emphasis. "Holly got the magic flower."

"Gus and I both got the flower," Holly corrected. "And he's the one who saved the cat."

"Your idea," Gus said. "I merely used gravity. Holly is the one who negotiated peace with a dragon. She got everyone talking while

I was still hiding. You should have seen her! The wizard was asleep, and the familiar was useless, but Holly was right in there, fearless. And the dragon was *huge!* Eat-you-in-one-bite huge."

"Spectacular!" Bluebell said, shaking his head so the pom-poms swayed. "Holly the Dragon Tamer!"

Holly giggled. That just sounded ridiculous. "He wasn't like what you'd think."

"Well, he sort of was," Gus said. "Large. Lots of fire. Bad-tempered."

"He was mostly misunderstood," Holly said.

Posing, Bluebell said, "You will be six — no, seven! — stanzas in my epic ballad. It will be glorious and stirring! First I begin with the Tale of the Flying Squirrel —"

Gus interrupted. "I'm sure it will be a fantastic ballad, but did the others succeed?"

"Very happy to report that we now possess four of the ingredients that the noble Charlie needs to recast the spell!" Bluebell announced. "Lavender the fox and Juniper the marmot succeeded in liberating the heart-shaped stone from the dormant volcano, while Pepper the flamingo and Tangerine the porcupine located the magic herb in the heart of a swamp."

"That's amazing!" Gus said.

"But that's not all! Dandelion the garter snake, with the help of our two mice friends, successfully retrieved the desert fruit that only ripens beneath the full moon."

"So that's four out of seven," Holly said. She felt so proud of her fellow shelterlings. "Only three more!" It had sounded nearly impossible when Charlie had described everything that had to be done, but already they were over halfway there!

"I shall continue composing my ballad, adding your stanzas," Bluebell declared. He hopped to the nest on the porch and pulled the brim of his hat over his eyes.

Holly carried the magic flower inside and, with Gus's help, found a pitcher and filled it with water. She put the flower in and admired it. It still looked as beautiful as it had the moment they'd plucked it, with its petals softly glowing. She positioned it on the kitchen table in the sunlight, safely away from the edge of the table in case anyone bumped into it.

Pepper poked her long neck into the kitchen. "Holly! Gus! You're back! And you have the flower! Yay!"

"I heard you got the magic herb," Gus said. "Congratulations!"

"I couldn't have done it without Tangerine," Pepper said. "You should have seen him! Or *not* seen him. Without his magic, he was camouflaged, brown on brown, in the swamp. When we got separated, I thought I'd be lost forever. But then he used his power: *anti*-camouflage! He was brilliant, both literally and figuratively. Bright orange against the endless brown mud. And then we got stuck in the mud . . ." She continued with a play-by-play of their adventure, which ended in finding and retrieving the magic herb that had grown where a bolt of lightning had struck. "And did you hear that Lavender and Juniper found the volcanic rock, and Dandelion, Briar, and Marble got the desert fruit?"

"We heard," Gus said. "It's fantastic! Charlie's going to be really proud of us."

We did it, Holly thought happily. *All of us.* "Where is he?"

"He's gone to Crescent City," Pepper said, "to ask the humans if they know where a star might have fallen. He said if he can narrow down the location, then Periwinkle should be able to use her power to pinpoint it exactly. Apparently, it's not easy to tell apart space rocks from ordinary rocks — that's why he needs her — but first she needs to know where to look."

Ah, that made sense. As Holly understood it, Periwinkle needed to be close enough to see a glow in order to find a lost object. "And Zephyr and Leaf?" They'd volunteered to retrieve the pearl from the saddest part of the sea. She expected them to be careening through the house, telling everyone who would listen about their adventure and bouncing off the walls. "Did they get the pearl?"

"They're not back yet," Pepper said.

That was surprising. Zephyr ran faster than any animal that Holly had ever seen, and they'd left before Holly and Gus. She would have expected them to be back days ago.

"I'm sure they'll succeed," Gus said.

Holly felt a twinge of concern. "I'm sure they will too. We need that pearl."

Charlie had been very clear about that — they needed to bring all the ingredients to the top of Cloud Mountain, or every stanza of Bluebell's ballad would be for nothing.

✦

Holly tried to hold on to the feeling of victory, but as the hours passed, she couldn't help the worries that began to creep in — it was all well and good to have found *some* of the ingredients, but for Charlie's plan to work, they needed *all* of them.

She spent their first day home watching out the window for Charlie to return with news about the fallen star or for Zephyr and Leaf to return with the pearl, and scurrying around the house and yard, neatening up.

The second day, she checked her acorn caches, counted all the acorns, and then counted them again. After she finished the second count, she poked her nose into Periwinkle's room. "Periwinkle, can I come in?"

"I didn't do it," the lemur said, her voice muffled.

Standing up on her hind legs, Holly tried to see her through the array of ribbons. "That's good," she said, though she had no idea what Periwinkle was referring to and wasn't sure she wanted to know. It could have just been an automatic response. "This is going to sound odd, but would you mind if I helped tidy up your treasures? I've run out of things to do." She'd been out in the yard, digging holes for her acorns, but she kept accidentally waking Gus, who was trying to sleep in the eaves of the house.

"You want to what?" Periwinkle asked. "Why?"

"It makes me feel better," Holly said. "And your room is a . . ." She didn't want to use the word "mess," but it was a hodgepodge of all the lost items that the lemur had accumulated. She saw a pyramid of sticks in the center, and pebbles strewn around. For all that Periwinkle called her found things treasures, she didn't seem to know how to keep them neat.

"It's *not* a mess," Periwinkle said.

"I wasn't going to say that."

"The others say it. They think I can't hear them. They call me a slob."

Holly began sweeping the pebbles into a pile with her tail. "You shouldn't listen to what they say. They just don't understand."

"And you do?"

"I hoard nuts. If you want to hoard pebbles and ribbons, who am I to criticize?" Methodically, she sorted through the pebbles by color and made a spiral of gray and another of white. After a few minutes, the lemur came out from between the ribbons to watch her.

It was soothing work, and it helped keep Holly from thinking about Zephyr and Leaf, or wondering if Charlie had had any luck in his search for a fallen star.

Silently, Periwinkle began to help, adding pebbles to the patterns.

In a very soft voice, Periwinkle said, "I put jam in Bluebell's hat."

For a second, Holly didn't know what she was talking about; then she remembered the jam stain on the ribbon. "He was the one eating too much jam."

"Yes, but later . . . He asked me to clean the spot because he said it was my fault. And it wasn't. So I thought that if I was going to be accused of it anyway, I might as well do it. And I put jam in his hat."

"Oh." Well, that wasn't the best choice. She tried to think of how to make it better. "Did you apologize?" she asked hopefully.

"I cleaned it off before he found out."

That . . . made it okay, didn't it? Sort of? "Glad to hear it."

"But I shouldn't have done it in the first place. It's just . . . He acts like he thinks he's so great. So much better than me. But he's in a place for mistakes too. No one wanted him, either."

"We wanted him," Holly said.

"But you don't want me," Periwinkle said. "You're just stuck with me."

Choosing her words carefully, Holly said, "We're still getting to know you. Most shelterlings are really friendly when given a chance. Maybe you could try being friendlier too. That would help." *Not dumping jam into anyone's hat would be a start*, she thought.

"Charlie keeps trying to be friendly," Periwinkle complained. "He keeps coming to my room to talk to me. What does he want from me?"

"Your help." He'd told the lemur that. They'd all heard. He had been very clear that he needed her special power to locate two of the seven ingredients.

"But why? Why does he need any of our help?"

"The spell requires seven ingredients —"

"He could have found them himself," Periwinkle said. "It's been less than a week, and you're already back with the flower, a snake and the mice with the fruit, the fox and the marmot with the whatever . . ."

"Heart-shaped rock from a volcano."

"Whatever. My point is: he could have done it himself. What does he need us for?"

It hadn't been *that* easy to pick the flower. She wondered if Charlie had known about the dragon and what he would have done if he'd been there. Or how he would have navigated the swamp to find the herb. *Not easy at all*, Holly thought. And Zephyr and Leaf still weren't back. She spared a moment to worry about them again. "It would have taken him weeks. Months."

"But why ask us? He could have asked real familiars."

That was true. Real familiars and wizards with all their proper magic might have found all seven ingredients by now . . . except that Saffron and his wizard hadn't been the one to persuade the dragon to cooperate. She and Gus had won the flower. If they hadn't come along, Saffron would still be caught in the golden net. His useful power hadn't been enough to save himself. "Maybe Charlie knew we could do it. He believes in us."

Periwinkle thought about that. "He believes in me?"

Holly nodded and said encouragingly, "I do too."

"Huh." Periwinkle fell silent, but she started sweeping the loose pebbles into a pile with her tail. Together, they neatened her room.

✦

The next morning, Zephyr and Leaf still weren't back.

Neither was Charlie.

Holly added more water to the pitcher with the magic flower. She studied it anxiously. The stem looked limp, and the petals were drooping.

In the other room, she heard the mice cleaning the kitchen floor, with the help of Dandelion. Another snake, Aster, was sweeping up tumbleweeds he'd accidentally summoned. She thought about going to lend him a paw, but then she heard Sparkles offering to help. So Holly stayed by the flower.

Gus was perched on the back of the chair behind her. "Stop fussing over it, Holly," he said. "It's just doing what cut flowers do."

Holly circled the flower a couple of times, viewing it from all angles. "What if it's not magic anymore? What if we ruined it?"

"We picked the right flower from the right place at the right time," Gus said. "Trust me, Charlie is going to be thrilled we got it. And he'll be thrilled about the other ingredients."

She sat back on her haunches and nibbled on a muffin she'd conjured. It was a blueberry-and-walnut muffin, with brown sugar topping. She offered a bite to Gus.

Four out of the seven, she thought. That was great, but what if Charlie couldn't locate the fallen star or the lost crystal? And what if Zephyr and Leaf couldn't retrieve the pearl?

Or, worse, what if they were in danger?

At last she blurted out, "Why aren't Zephyr and Leaf back yet?" It had been too many days, and the ocean wasn't nearly as far away as the cliffs had been. Pearl or no pearl, they should have returned by now.

"Oh, I see." He spread his wing out and then refolded them.

"That's what you're really worried about. Not the flower. You think something could have happened to them?"

Surely Zephyr and Leaf were just being slow. *But Zephyr is never slow,* she thought. Anything could have happened. She and Gus had run into a dragon, for goodness' sake. The possibilities were endless. But she didn't want to say any of that out loud. "I am worried the petals are drooping." She wondered if she should add anything to the water. Sugar maybe? She knew there was a jar of sugar on the third shelf in the kitchen. She could try a sprinkle —

"Do you want to do something about it?" Gus asked.

"I could try some sugar . . ."

"I mean about Zephyr and Leaf."

Holly looked over at Gus, hoping he was suggesting what she thought he was. They couldn't do anything to help Charlie in the city. But maybe Zephyr and Leaf . . .

Gus spread his wings again. "So long as you aren't tired of flying . . ."

"Never," she said. "Let's go!"

CHAPTER NINE

Holly and Gus flew east, toward the sun and the sea, over a patchwork of farmland. They soared above sheep, cows, and horses, as well as over crops of wheat and corn. Sometimes they saw farmers in their fields or in carts on the roads. Holly wondered what the humans thought of a squirrel flying on the back of an owl — if they even looked up to see — and then decided it didn't matter what anyone thought. She loved flying.

"We should fly like this all the time," Holly said into Gus's ear.

"Sure," he said. "No reason why we can't."

Huh . . . She supposed that was true.

She mulled it over in her head. She'd believed that once the wizards rejected her, that was it for her dreams of adventuring. Mistakes weren't supposed to go on journeys. They were supposed to stay out of sight. But now that she thought of it . . . no one had ever specifically said, No, *you can't travel if you aren't a familiar.* She'd just always assumed that, since the wizards had dismissed her, she couldn't.

Yet here she was, and it wasn't as if anyone was interested in stopping her. The farmers below hadn't even noticed her, and the birds in the sky — the sparrows, the swallow, the hawks — were flapping about on their own business, consumed in their own lives.

Maybe I could have been flying like this all along, she thought.

She was still thinking about that when she saw the sea.

The blue grew bigger and bigger, until it filled her entire view, pale blue for the sky and deep blue for the sea. She'd never imagined so much blue! It was as if a pond had started eating and hadn't known when to stop and so had kept growing until it had swallowed the world. "Wow, it looks endless!"

"It makes you feel small, doesn't it?" Gus said.

It . . . didn't, actually. It made her feel as though if she spread her paws out, she could hold the entire world between her claws.

As they flew closer, she saw the waves curling into themselves as they ran toward the shore, and then collapsing in a spray of white foam. She smelled the salty air, carried on the wind, and she heard the crunching crash of the waves on the sand.

"Now what? How are we supposed to find Zephyr and Leaf in all this?" It had seemed like such a reasonable idea: fly to the sea and help the turtle and the gecko. But now that she saw how vast it was . . . She'd heard the expression "looking for a needle in a haystack," and — setting aside the question of why anyone would put a needle in a haystack in the first place — this felt similar. There was so much blue.

"Look for the rock in the sea with a diamond-shaped hole in its center," Gus said. "Remember what Charlie said? He figured out that the kind of pearl we want grows in oysters that live in a shipwreck — the saddest part of the sea — and there's a sunken ship that's supposed to be near that rock."

"You're a genius." She hadn't absorbed all the details. She'd been too distracted by the thought of fixing the Moon Mirror to listen.

Gus shrugged his feathery shoulders as he flew. "I just pay attention."

He dipped lower, and she heard the waves louder. The sound reminded her of a heartbeat, steady, as if the ocean itself were alive. She looked in both directions as the salty air ruffled her fur. North, the sandy shore stretched unbroken as far as she could see, but south had rocky cliffs that cut the farmland off from the ocean. "Do you know which direction the rock is?" Holly asked.

"Yep. Listened to that, too." He soared south, following the shoreline.

She scanned the water as they flew. Several rocks jutted out of the waves. Seagulls perched on top of them. None of the rocks had holes of any kind that Holly could see. She wondered what size hole Charlie had been talking about.

Beside them, the waves lapped the shore. Seagulls cried to one another, hoarse calls that sounded like insults but were really saying "Nice day."

It *was* a nice day, even though she was worried about Zephyr and Leaf. She felt lucky to be here, flying with Gus. Especially lucky that he knew the way. He'd paid close attention. She wondered why he'd cared so much. She knew why *she* wanted to help

Charlie cast his spell — a chance to be a familiar instead of just an oddball squirrel — and she knew a lot of the other animals felt the same way. But Gus had never dreamed of becoming a familiar, not really. He'd told her he'd climbed the mountain not because he wanted to be a familiar but because he didn't want to be a solitary owl anymore. He'd been lonely in his home forest, where everyone expected owls to keep to themselves. Drinking from the Moon Mirror had been a way to change things. "Gus . . . why are you helping Charlie with his plan?"

"Why? Because I like the smell of the sea."

Holly felt spray on her fur. Drops clung to her whiskers as Gus rose back up into the air. She shook her whiskers and laughed. "Really, Gus, I'm serious. You've never talked about wanting more magic."

"I'm not doing this to be an owl with flashier magic."

"Then why?"

"Because Charlie's plan gives me the chance to make all my friends happy," Gus said.

Before she could think of a response that felt special enough for such a sweet statement, she spotted their destination: the rock with the diamond-shaped hole.

She'd pictured a rock like the kind one saw in the pasture behind the shelter: taller than a turtle but shorter than a cow. This, however, was a massive, craggy outcropping. It glistened with seawater and was rough with barnacles. Waves crashed in white foam around it, spraying the diamond-shaped opening in its center. She could see blue water and blue sky through the diamond, as if it were a window.

They flew toward it.

Closer, Holly leaned forward against Gus's feathery neck, trying to see if there was anyone within the window. The ocean rolled beneath them as Gus soared nearer.

"I see them!" he cried.

She squinted.

But a squirrel's vision wasn't as sharp as an owl's, and it was only when they were nearly there that she spotted the unmistakable curve of a turtle's back within the diamond. She couldn't tell if Leaf was with him, but he had to be. The two were inseparable, like her and Gus. "Zephyr!" she called. "Hello!"

"Hello? Who said that?" Zephyr called.

Gus circled the rock and then landed on top. Holly slid off his back and scurried down the side of the rock until she reached the turtle. "Zephyr, we were worried about you!" she chittered. "Where's Leaf? Is he okay?"

The gecko poked his tiny head over the top of Zephyr's shell. "Fine. Except we're trapped on this rock. And I, for one, am not a fan of being trapped on a rock in the middle of the ocean!" His voice rose louder and louder with each word.

"It's not my fault," Zephyr said.

"In what way is this not your fault?" Leaf said. "'Don't swim out to the rock,' I said. 'You're a freshwater turtle, not a sea turtle,' I said. 'Swimming in the ocean might be different from swimming in a pond. There might be waves. There might be sharks. There might be whales, eels, octopi, and other turtle-eating animals.' But did you listen? No, you did not. Do you ever listen to me? No, you do not. And so here we are. In the sea. On this rock. Stuck."

"Can't you just puff up and float to shore?" Gus asked.

"(A) I'm not leaving Zephyr," Leaf said, "and (B) there's too much wind. I can't fight against wind." He wiggled his feet. He used them to steer when he floated. They were strong enough to keep him from floating up to the clouds and nimble enough to maneuver around the shelter, but not powerful enough to resist the kind of wind that was blowing across the ocean. "I'd blow out to sea."

"If you'd practiced more, maybe you could —" Zephyr said.

"Little feet! And too much wind!" Leaf said, sticking a foot in Zephyr's face and wiggling his toes again. "Besides, it's a bit too late for practicing now."

Holly frowned, thinking. "But if Zephyr swam out here, why can't he just swim back?"

"Look down," Leaf said.

The owl waddled to the edge and peered into the water. Holly walked over next to him, careful to keep her paws spread wide so she wouldn't slip, and looked down too. Spray spat in her face. The seawater, she thought, tasted like soup made by someone who didn't know how to make soup.

"What do you see?" Leaf asked.

"Water," Gus said. "Lots of it."

"Super helpful. Can you see anything *in* the water?"

Gus leaned farther over the edge. "The water is darker over here. I think that means it's deeper."

"And . . . ?" Leaf prompted.

"And lots more water?" Holly said.

"*And a giant fish!*" Leaf shrieked.

Looking again, Holly didn't see any fish, just seaweed swept by the waves.

"Believe me, it's down there," Leaf said. "That fish is the reason that we can't swim back to shore. And the reason we can't get the pearl."

"I was going to dive for it," Zephyr said. "I can hold my breath for twenty-seven minutes, give or take a few, so I was sure I'd be able to do it. I had a cousin who could hold her breath for forty-three minutes. It was her party trick."

"But then we saw the giant fish who wants to eat turtles and geckos for lunch," Leaf said. "No one's diving in that water. Not for even the most magical pearl in the world."

"There must be a way to get it," Holly said. "We need it."

"I'll be happy if we can just get off this rock," Leaf said glumly.

"And eat," Zephyr said. "Sure, normal turtles can last six months without food, but I'm a *fast* turtle! All I can think about is lettuce."

"We're hungry, we're tired, and we just want to go home," Leaf said.

Holly swished her tail back and forth. "But the pearl!"

"Some other animal is going to have to get it," Leaf said. "We failed. That shouldn't be a surprise, though. We're failures."

They couldn't give up! Maybe if Zephyr tried to dive faster, or if they distracted the fish, or . . . But as Holly looked at Zephyr and Leaf, she knew that they were done. "How long have you been stuck here?"

"Days," Leaf said. "Too many days."

"We found the rock right away," Zephyr said. "And then —"

"Giant fish."

"We were lucky it rained," Zephyr said. "So we had fresh water. But no lettuce. No leaves. No grass. No worms. No berries." Leaf bobbed his head fervently.

"Then the most important thing is to get you off this rock," Holly said decidedly. The pearl could wait. Helping her friends came first. Stuffing down her disappointment, she stared into the water. Surely a fish couldn't be *that* scary.

"How do you know it's not friendly?" Holly asked. After all, even the unfriendly dragon had been willing to negotiate. This giant fish could be the same. She wondered if they'd tried.

"It's *not* a friendly fish," Leaf said.

"He's right," Zephyr said glumly. "I tried to dive down to the shipwreck when we first got here, and it chased me back to the surface. Not very fun."

"But you're the fastest turtle alive!" Gus said. "Can't you escape an ordinary fish?"

"Sure, an ordinary fish," Zephyr said, "but this —"

Leaf jumped in. "I don't think you understand exactly how big it is. You know Clover?"

Holly chittered as she imagined a fish the size of a cow. "It's that big?"

"It's as big as *three* cows," Zephyr said.

She tried to imagine that and failed. He had to be exaggerating. She'd expected a dragon to be enormous, but a *fish?* Surely that couldn't be right. She'd had a stream running through her forest, and she'd heard of salmon growing up to sixty inches long. But three times a cow?

"I'm fast, but that monster is like a train in the water. I can't outrun a train!"

Leaf scurried to the opposite side of the rock. His grippy toes were spread wide, and he swung his head from side to side. Occasionally, he tasted the air with his tongue. His skinny tail wrapped around a barnacle. "It's hopeless."

"Hey now," Gus said, "that's a bit grim."

"How do you know it's still here?" Holly asked. She peered down into the water again. She saw minnows dart in schools, zigzagging through the water, but no leviathan. "Maybe it's gone."

"Doubt it," Leaf said.

"But you don't know," Holly pointed out. "I can't see it."

"Me either," Gus said. "And I have excellent eyesight."

The turtle stuck his head farther out of the shell. "If it left, then I should try again."

"Wait, wait, wait, we don't know that it's gone," Leaf said. "What if that monstrosity sees us again? We barely made it to the rock, and you want to take another risk?"

"I have to try. I can't stay here any longer. Like you said, Leaf, I'm hungry, tired, and homesick." Zephyr scooted to the edge of the rock and looked out across the waves toward shore as if calculating the distance. Holly looked too. She'd seen how fast he could run. If he swam at his usual superspeed, he could reach the shore before the giant fish returned. "Are you coming?" he asked Leaf.

Leaf scurried onto Zephyr's shell and gripped the edge. "Just to be clear, I want it known that I disapprove." Nervously, he licked his eyeball.

"Be careful, both of you," Holly said.

Zephyr revved up his back legs, then raced down the rock toward the water. "Hang on!"

"Go, Zephyr!" Holly shouted. "You can do it!"

He swam, speeding through the water. "Woo-hoo!" Zephyr cried as he rode the waves. Gus and Holly cheered.

"Watch out for the fish!" Leaf cried.

And a black-and-white whale rose out of the water, its toothy mouth open wide.

Chapter Ten

As Holly shouted and Gus shrieked, Zephyr braked in the water. Spray from the turtle's feet spurted up in the whale's face.

With Leaf clinging to his shell, Zephyr sped back toward the rock.

"Faster!" Holly shouted to Zephyr.

He's not going to make it, she thought.

The whale dived back beneath the waves. Its tail flicked upward. Holly spotted it rising again. Its dorsal fin sliced through the water.

And then, to her horror, she realized that she could no longer see Leaf — the spot on the turtle's shell where the little gecko had clung was empty. She scampered up the side of the rock, trying to see better. "Leaf! Where's Leaf?" Had he slipped off? Was he in the water?

"Leaf!" Zephyr cried.

From above, Leaf shouted back, "I'm here!" Floating several feet above the waves, the gecko had puffed into a balloon shape. He drifted, buffeted by the ocean wind. He stretched out his tiny feet helplessly. "Go faster!"

"You've never . . ." Zephyr puffed as he swam, "told me . . . to go faster." Puff, puff. "You always . . . tell me . . . to slow down."

All of them screamed, "Faster!"

The whale burst out of the water inches behind Zephyr. Its mouth was wide, its many teeth gleaming, its broad tongue ready to scoop up the turtle —

Holly yelled at the massive creature, "Stop! Or we'll . . ." As Leaf drifted by, she had a burst of inspiration. "Or we'll pluck you out of the ocean and make you float like that lizard!" Shaking her paw, she chittered at the whale. "We'd do it! And you wouldn't like it! Not one bit!"

Surprised, it paused to look at Holly.

Seizing the moment, Zephyr spurted forward and, speeding up a wave as if it were a ramp, launched himself toward the rock. He belly-flopped onto the bottom of the rock, and Gus flew down. Using his talons, the owl hauled the turtle up to the safety of the opening.

"Are you okay?" Holly asked, running in circles around Zephyr.

He pulled his head back into his shell. "I nearly lost Leaf. My best friend."

Gus flapped back up to the top of the rock and perched above them. "Leaf is fine."

"I am not fine," the gecko said as he floated, balloon-shaped, past the diamond hole in the rock. "I am most definitely freaked out." Only his snout and toes stuck out, making him an imperfect sphere. He wiggled his toes — angrily, Holly thought.

"Think calm thoughts!" she called to the round gecko.

"As soon as we're safe on shore, I'll tell you exactly what my thoughts are!" A puff of wind tumbled him head over tail, and he somersaulted as the waves swelled beneath him. "I absolutely never thought I'd say this," he said to Zephyr, "but you weren't fast enough."

"I tried to get us there," Zephyr said, still within his shell. "I did my best."

Gawking at the waves, Gus said, "Not your fault. That was . . . I don't know what that was, but it was *not* a fish."

"It's an orca," Holly said. "Also known as a killer whale." Now that she'd gotten a good look, she was sure of it. Pepper had told her about them, when Holly had asked her for stories about the ocean. Its black-and-white face was unmistakable. Pepper had said that orcas preferred northern waters but could live anywhere, and that they ate just about anything: fish, seals, birds, dolphins, even great white sharks. And turtles.

Quieting, the squirrel, turtle, gecko, and owl watched the orca as it churned the water, rolling in the waves and slapping the ocean with its fins. It dived and rose and bobbed, as if it didn't want them to forget it was there.

As if we could *forget it's there*, Holly thought.

Compared to the four shelterlings on the rock, the killer whale was a true leviathan. It was also beautiful. Its black-and-white flanks glistened as it rose and dived and spun. The sea danced around the creature as if the water were obeying its commands.

"You know, it's not a terrible idea," Gus said.

"What isn't?" Holly asked.

"I don't mean lifting an orca," Gus began.

"Good," Leaf said, still floating, "because that *is* a terrible idea."

And an impossible one, Holly knew. The gecko wasn't much larger than the orca's eye. There was zero way he could lift a killer whale out of the water, no matter what Holly had threatened.

"Lift Zephyr," Gus said.

"What? Me lift him?" Leaf said. "Okay, yes, he's lighter than an orca, but still! And even if I could, how would that work?" He flapped his tiny hands. "Wind, remember? We'd both be blown out to sea."

"You provide the buoyancy," Gus said, "and I'll provide the thrust."

Excited, Holly ran in a tight circle, keeping to the heart of the rock. "Yes! Both of you, working together! You can do it!" She knew Gus was strong. She'd seen him lift stones out of the garden that must have weighed at least six or seven pounds.

"It will help if we can start as high up as possible," Gus said. "That way we won't have to raise him higher to clear the waves. All we'll have to do is fly straight to shore. Zephyr, can you climb to the top of the rock?"

"Yes! Absolutely! Maybe."

"Turtles aren't known as climbers," Leaf said.

"But that doesn't mean I can't be one," Zephyr said. "If I try."

They urged him on as he began his climb — not an easy feat for a turtle. Holly zipped around him, coaxing him upward, helping him find the least slippery crevasses for his wide feet. Gus swooped through the air, calling out advice: "Left leg! That's it! No, not there! Yes, there!"

Leaf, meanwhile, continued to float and complain. "I don't like this. What if we can't hold him? What if he falls? What if we drop him right into the orca's mouth? I'd never forgive myself."

"Hush," Zephyr puffed. "I can't just stay here."

"We could," Leaf said. "Gus could bring us food. It's a nice view."

Holly glared at him. "Leaf. It's a rock."

Zephyr reached with one of his short legs, and his hind leg slipped. Scurrying around him, Holly tried to — well, she didn't know what she was trying to do. She didn't think. She instinctively ran beneath him to catch him, and when he started to fall, he bumped into her and she lost her grip.

Her paws scrambled in the air, and all of a sudden she felt only wind around her.

It happened too fast for her to even scream.

With a whoosh, Gus swooped under her, and she fell into the softness of his feathers. He rose up above the waves and the orca and deposited her on the top of the rock.

She clung to the rock with all four paws, her heart racing so fast that she felt as if it were humming inside her chest. "Zephyr?" she managed to ask.

With a grunt, the turtle heaved himself up onto the top of the rock. He lifted his head. "Made it. I'm ready. Leaf?"

A thin voice answered, but it was too far away for Holly to hear the words. The wind had carried Leaf farther out to sea. "Gus —" she said.

But Gus was already flying toward the drifting gecko.

He reached him while Holly and Zephyr watched. The little gecko grabbed onto the owl's feathers and then was so relieved that he deflated. As Gus flew back to the rock, Holly marveled at her friend. He'd flown her all the way here, saved her from her fall, saved Leaf from drifting out to sea, and was game to attempt rescuing Zephyr from being stranded on this rock.

How could the wizards have refused him? They'd missed out on a true hero. And for that, Holly was grateful. If they'd accepted Gus, she never would have met her best friend.

With Leaf, Gus landed back on the rock. The gecko scurried down and ran to Zephyr. "This is a bad idea," Leaf said. "I really think we should seriously consider just living here forever." He huddled against the rock, shivering with either cold or fear — Holly couldn't tell which.

"I thought you wanted to help," Holly said.

"I do! But . . ."

"Just inflate," Gus urged him.

He wailed. "I can't! I can't concentrate! I can't —"

In a burst of inspiration, Holly knew exactly what to do. It wasn't *nice*, precisely, but . . . Swinging her tail, she whacked at the little lizard. He slipped from the side of the rock. Shrieking, he instantly inflated.

"Sorry," Holly said.

He scrambled his little hands and feet in the air. "Holly! That was —"

"Brilliant," Gus said. "Now let's save our friend, okay?" He used his wings to create a burst of wind that sent Leaf floating toward the turtle. "Zephyr! Grab on!"

"Not the tail!" Leaf cried.

Zephyr clamped his turtle beak around one of Leaf's tiny legs, and Gus gripped Zephyr's shell with his talons. Starting from the top of the rock, they had the best angle for takeoff. Flapping, he soared off the rock.

Leaf squawked.

For a second they sank, and then Gus flapped harder.

"I'll be back for you, Holly," he told her.

She rose up onto her hind legs and watched them fly, rising and sinking, toward the shore. Below, the orca swam. But her friends continued to fly, several feet above the waves.

She felt so proud that she wanted to sing. *They're going to make it!* Granted, they'd failed to retrieve the pearl, but at least —

"Fascinating," a voice chirped.

She didn't know where the voice had come from. Twisting, she scanned the sky. No seabirds. And then she looked down at the sea. The orca had raised its head out of the water, vertically, bobbing in the waves. Sunlight gleamed on its water-slick, smooth black-and-white face.

"Birds I have seen, but a turtle flying? I suppose technically he isn't so much flying as being flown. Still, I wouldn't have guessed it was possible. Turtles are dense. And meaty. Yum."

"He has wonderful friends," Holly said. "That's how it's possible."

"Tasty friends?" the orca wondered.

Holly saw Gus falter, and they dipped toward the waves. Quickly she said, "Oh no, they taste terrible. That species of turtle tastes like licorice. And the owl tastes like a swamp."

"I've never tried either," the orca said. "Perhaps I'd like them."

"You'd be sick," Holly warned. "Upset stomach. Bellyache. Also, the lizard would make you vomit. You wouldn't like that, especially in the water. It would be a mess."

The orca swam closer to the rock. "How do *you* taste, little fuzzy thing?"

"I'm a squirrel," Holly said. "And I'm inedible too. Venomous. That's . . . um, what my fluffy tail signifies. Unsafe to eat."

"Usually venom is signaled by bright colors."

"Ha! Well, I'm an unusual squirrel?" She winced at herself. Out over the water, a gust of wind knocked the owl, turtle, and gecko to the side. Hoping to keep the orca's attention on her — and away from her vulnerable friends — Holly changed the subject. "So you're an orca. I've never met an orca before!"

"And I have never met a venomous squirrel," the orca said. "So pleased that I left my pod to investigate. What an unusual group of creatures." Its gaze shifted back to Gus, Zephyr, and Leaf.

They were dipping lower and lower toward the waves.

"You know, I could just nip over there —"

Holly jumped in. "Tell me about your pod. You said you have one. Is it . . . um . . . ." She didn't know what to ask that would distract the orca from her possible snack. ". . . a lot of orcas?"

"It is my grandmother's pod," the orca said. "She leads us.

When she is too old, it will be my mother's pod, and then it will be mine. Right now, there are fifteen of us. The others were hunting sea lions, but I spotted the fast turtle and his friend and came to investigate." Again, her attention drifted back to Holly's friends. "I have encountered puffer fish who can expand to be spherical, but never a lizard. How is he doing it?"

The owl flapped harder, and they rose up. She wished they'd rise even higher. Holly didn't know how high a killer whale could jump, but she guessed it was higher than they were flying. "Magic. That's his special power."

"Intriguing." The orca rolled onto her side and then bobbed up again, as if she were standing in the water. "Tell me more. How does this lizard have magic?"

"He's a gecko. And he drank from a magic pool."

They dipped again, flying much too low. If the orca lunged forward, she'd be able to snap them all out of the air with ease. "A pool that grants creatures magic?" the orca asked.

I have to keep her distracted, Holly thought, *until Gus gets everyone to shore.*

Holly told the killer whale everything: how the magic water on Cloud Mountain gave you powers, how the shelterlings' powers were broken, and how they were trying to fix the Moon Mirror with a spell. The orca had question after question — the idea of magic seemed to fascinate her. Holly tried to answer in as much detail as possible, to buy her friends as much time as possible. She told her everything she knew about Charlie's discovery and how he'd painstakingly researched a spell and learned of the seven special ingredients. "That's why we're here," Holly said. "We need a pearl from the ocean floor near this rock so we can fix our magic."

"Your magic seems to work well enough," the orca said. "The turtle is the fastest of his kind I have ever chased. That is why he interested me in the first place." She pivoted again to watch Holly's friends.

Only a little farther . . .

Come on, Gus, Zephyr, Leaf! You can make it! Out loud, Holly asked, "You chased him because you're curious?

"Curious. Hungry. What other reason is there to do anything?" the orca asked.

It was always this way talking with carnivores outside the shelter. They just couldn't seem to help mentioning their appetite. The orca, however, seemed to particularly relish talking about it. "Kindness," Holly answered. "Friendship."

"We haven't met," the orca pointed out. "We aren't friends."

"My name is Holly. What's yours?"

"Cerulean," the orca said.

"That's a beautiful name. And now we're friends." She wasn't sure that was true, but she'd rather the orca think of her as Holly than as lunch.

"So . . . friend . . . tell me, why do you need this pearl if you already have magic?" She said the word "magic" as if she were tasting it and found it as sweet as sugar.

"I told you, our power is all messed up," Holly said. "Gus can only turn to stone. Leaf puffs up like a balloon. And Zephyr is fast and strong, but his reflexes are still turtle slow. No wizard wants a familiar with magic like ours."

"Like yours? What is your power, little niblet?"

"Holly," she corrected. "I can only conjure pastries." It was the least useful power she could think of, especially out here in the ocean. Concentrating, she demonstrated. A raspberry Danish appeared in her hand. She tossed it toward the water, and Cerulean caught it in her mouth. It looked tiny on her vast tongue.

The orca swallowed. "Unusual."

"That's a polite way to put it."

"But I still don't understand. You can conjure treats out of thin air. Why do you need a wizard?" the orca asked. "I have seen them on their ships, trying to control the wind. A dour lot. Always so serious. Not tasty-looking at all."

"If you bond with a wizard, you have a purpose," Holly said. "You accompany them on their quests and help them achieve heroic acts that make the world a better place. It's a noble way of life. And it's the only way for an animal to have a different life from the one he or she was born into."

"'The only way'? You believe you cannot achieve heroic acts on your own, little niblet? Have you tried? And kept trying? My grandmother tells our pod: You are only a failure if you quit. Until then, you're just a creature who hasn't succeeded *yet*."

Holly thought of Saffron and the dragon and wasn't sure what to say. Saffron had acted as if she'd done something heroic. He'd certainly been glad she hadn't quit when they saw the golden web or when they saw the enormous dragon.

"Your friend, the little puffer fish who is not a fish — he got his magic the same way you did? And the turtle?" the orca asked. "Can anyone drink this magic water?"

"Yes, they did, and yes, anyone can. It's open to any creature who wants magic." She hesitated, because she realized it wasn't strictly true. It was open to anyone who could reach the Moon Mirror, but ocean creatures didn't have that option. "Or at least any creature who can make the trek to the top of Cloud Mountain . . ."

"Which I cannot," Cerulean finished for her. "Well, then, this has been fascinating, but I can see my lunch has nearly gotten away, and so —"

Thinking fast, Holly called to her, "What if you could have magic?"

The orca paused. "Go on, little niblet."

It seemed ridiculous. What would a creature as massive and powerful as Cerulean want with magic? But the orca was clearly fascinated by magic, and it was the only idea Holly had. She had to try. "Would you want it? If you could?"

The orca ducked beneath the surface and then bobbed up again. "I would."

"You'd want to be a familiar? But you said wizards are dour."

"I don't want a wizard." The orca swam closer to the rock. "Unless they're delicious."

"Then why —"

The orca said, "I want *magic*." She purred the word.

If the orca wanted magic without a wizard, who was Holly to say she had to have one? After all, no one had ever said you *must* bond with a wizard. Just that you *should*. And really, did it matter *why* the orca wanted magic? What mattered was that Holly had something to bargain with.

"If you don't eat me or my friends . . . and if you bring me the pearl . . . then after we've fixed the Moon Mirror, I'll bring you some of its water," Holly promised.

"Intriguing." The orca swam in a circle, her fin cutting through the waves. "How can I trust you will fulfill your side of the bargain?"

"What do you have to lose?" Holly countered.

"A tasty snack."

Conjuring a croissant, Holly tossed it to her. The orca caught it and swallowed it. "I promise I'll bring you the magic water. I'm a trustworthy squirrel. I always help my friends, and we're friends now, Cerulean." She said it with as much confidence as she could, and she meant every word.

"I will bring you the pearl," the orca said.

And the killer whale dived beneath the waves.

CHAPTER ELEVEN

Running from one side of the rock to the other, Holly watched the surface of the sea. The wet barnacles felt rough on her paws, reminding her of bark on a pine tree after a rainfall. Above, a seagull squawked at her, curious why a squirrel was out at sea. Intent on the waves, she didn't answer it.

Flying closer, it squawked again, this time asking if she had food.

"Shoo," Gus said to the gull as he landed back on top of the rock.

With a rude response, the gull flew off.

"I've heard they steal food," Gus said, shaking out his wings. He preened his feathers before looking down at her. "Ready to go?"

"Not yet," she said.

"What do you mean, 'not yet'? Zephyr and Leaf are safe on shore."

"Not yet," she repeated. "I'm waiting for the orca. Trust me."

"Always," Gus said.

The sun was high overhead, and the ocean sparkled. Holly watched for shadows between the waves. The sea wasn't just one shade of blue, she noticed — it varied from white, when the waves hit the rock, to a thick-with-seaweed dark blue, to black at its deepest. She wondered what else was down there, aside from killer whales and sunken ships and magic pearls.

Maybe when this is all over, I can ask Cerulean, she thought.

"Are you ready now?"

"She's not back yet." Holly scurried to the eastern edge of the rock and peered down, then switched to the western edge. The blueness was impenetrable, even by the sun, and the foam crashing onto the rocks further obscured her view.

"Isn't that a good thing?"

She realized he'd misunderstood — he thought she was waiting to make sure the orca was gone. "We made an arrangement." She explained the deal she'd offered Cerulean. There were details to be worked out — how to carry the water, how to give it to the orca without spilling it in the sea — but that was for later.

"That's brilliant, Holly. Do you think she'll —"

The orca surfaced, and Cerulean swam closer to the rock. Holly scurried over, while Gus let out a warning hoot. "Holly, be careful."

"Did you find it?" Holly asked.

"The oyster volunteered it as soon as I asked. It bothered him, he said. He arranged for a crab to deliver it to me. And now I'm delivering it to you." Cerulean opened her mouth wide. Lying on her tongue was what looked like a perfectly round stone. It was iridescently white, and it glistened in the sunlight. Holly stretched out her paw, but she couldn't reach.

"Holly . . ." Gus said.

"Can I trust you?" Holly asked the orca.

"Friends trust friends," Cerulean said — which, Holly thought, wasn't precisely an answer.

Did she trust Cerulean? The whole time Gus, Zephyr, and Leaf had been flying to shore, the orca had considered eating them . . . but curiosity had drawn her, not just hunger. And when Holly had talked about magic, she'd seemed even more curious. Holly recognized that kind of curiosity — a curiosity that was like hunger. She'd felt it when she'd first heard about the magic water. She used to gobble up any and all stories about the Moon Mirror and about familiars with their wizards. And Cerulean *had* chosen to retrieve the pearl rather than eat Holly's friends. That spoke volumes.

Besides, if she didn't trust the killer whale, she wouldn't get the pearl. And she needed that pearl if she ever wanted to be like Calla, Emerald, or Quill.

Climbing over Cerulean's teeth, she crawled into the killer whale's mouth. Very aware of the teeth and the orca's hot fish breath, Holly picked up the pearl with her front paws and then hurried back onto the rock.

She held it up for Gus to see —

And the seagull swooped down and plucked it out of her paws.

"No!" she yelled at it. "Give that back!" She scurried up the side of the rock to the top, where Gus was perched.

He launched into the air. "Return that pearl!"

More gulls swooped in. They screeched, "Food! Everyone, we found food! Come quick! We have food!"

"It's not food!" Holly yelled.

Gus flew at the gulls, but there were too many of them. They sniped at him with their beaks, and he retreated, shouting at them to return the pearl.

From the ocean, Cerulean said, "Use your magic."

Her magic had never helped with anything. Conjuring pastries was a useless power. *But it's exactly what the gulls want*, she realized. She should listen to the orca.

"You want food?" Holly called. "How about this?" Concentrating, she summoned a croissant. She tossed it into the air. Two gulls swooped and grabbed it, ripping it apart. Crumbs sprayed into the sky and floated like confetti down onto the rock.

More gulls swooped toward the crumbs.

"Give us the pearl, and I'll give you more," Holly said.

One of the gulls poked her with his beak. "Where do you have more? You're not carrying more." He prodded her again. "I can't smell more."

"I can make you more," she said, swatting him back. "Do you want another croissant? Or how about a muffin? Do you like muffins? Tell me any kind of baked good, and you can have it. Just give us the pearl."

"You can't eat the pearl anyway," Gus said.

"Give us each a muffin," the gull said. "And swear that we don't have to share them with you."

"They're all yours," Holly promised.

Concentrating, she imagined a plump blueberry muffin, with sugar on top. The smell curled up toward her nose, and she felt the heavy weight suddenly pop into her hands. She laid it on the rock. She kept conjuring baked goods until there was a muffin for each gull.

"Marvelous," Cerulean said.

"Now the pearl!" Holly ordered.

The gull with the pearl opened its beak, and the pearl fell toward Holly. Scurrying underneath it, she held up her paws and caught it.

Gus flew down, and she jumped off the rock onto his back, with the pearl in her paws.

"Good luck, little niblet!" Cerulean called. "Remember your promise! Bring me *magic!*"

"I'll be back!" Holly promised. "Thank you!"

The orca submerged, and Gus and Holly flew toward the shore, as the gulls gorged themselves on the muffins she'd left behind on the rock in the sea.

✦

Holly and Gus flew toward home, while Zephyr and Leaf ran beneath them. It didn't take long for the speedy turtle and his passenger to outrun them, but Holly didn't mind. As the turtle shrank to a dot on the horizon and then disappeared, she enjoyed the flight.

Gus was clutching the pearl in his talons so that she could hold on to his feathers.

She wished they could fly forever. But eventually they flew over farms and fields that she knew she'd seen before. As they soared high above empty train tracks, she lifted her face to feel the wind in her fur. And then, sooner than she would have liked, below was the shelter, with its gardens and orchards.

Gus glided between the peonies and landed. He released the pearl, and she picked it up. "Thanks for flying all this way," Holly said. "You must be tired."

"I may sleep for a month."

"You don't hibernate."

"I think I'm going to start," he said. "I'll be a new breed of hibernating owl."

Holly laughed and watched as Gus flew up into the eaves of the house and settled onto a perch. He folded his wings and nestled his beak against his chest.

She smiled up at him and then climbed onto the porch.

Before she reached the door, Charlie burst out of the house. "Do you have it?"

With her tail proudly raised behind her, she held up the pearl in her front paws. It shimmered softly with a moonlike sheen. She thought it was one of the most perfect objects she'd ever seen. And she'd succeeded in bringing this prize home.

He took it and held it up so it glowed in the sunlight. "Oh, well done, Holly, my favorite squirrel!" He thumped his broad beaver tail on the porch as if applauding. "Zephyr and Leaf told me how brave and clever you were."

"I couldn't have done it without them or Gus."

"That's not what Zephyr and Leaf said. You negotiated with a killer whale!" He patted her shoulder with one paw while hugging the pearl with his other. "So proud of you. First a dragon, now a whale. I didn't know you had it in you. I'm going to show this pearl to everyone. They'll be so happy to see it. And I know they'll be just as proud of you as I am."

Holly beamed at him. She didn't think anyone had ever been proud of her before, except Gus. She liked how it made her feel: all warm inside, as if she'd been lying out in the summer sun. She imagined herself, surrounded by all her friends, climbing to the top of Cloud Mountain, and how proud she'd feel then.

"Do we have all the ingredients?" she asked.

"Only two left, and those are the ones I need Periwinkle's help for — the piece of a fallen star and the crystal in the hidden cave," Charlie said. "I'm still working on locating the cave, but I've tracked down a rumor of where a bit of a star hit the earth. Now I need Periwinkle to complete the job. And that's why I must ask for your help again, Holly."

"Me? You just said you need Periwinkle."

"I need you to talk to her," Charlie said. "For me. For all of us. We're so close, Holly! All our dreams can come true! But only if we all work together. And right now, she's refusing."

"Refusing? Why?" She knew Periwinkle had been prickly in the beginning, when Charlie had first explained his plan, but surely now, after they'd returned with so many ingredients and she'd seen how much it mattered to everyone . . .

"I don't know why she's refusing, but I was hoping you'd talk with her."

Charlie should really be the one to talk to Periwinkle, Holly thought. After all, he was the one who had united all of them in this endeavor. He was the one all the shelterlings looked up to and depended on. Except that he was looking at Holly as if *he* depended on *her*. "What happened?"

"I tried to explain what she needs to do, and now she's refusing to come out of her ribbon-festooned room. I don't understand it. I must have said something wrong, but I don't know what." She heard the frustration in his voice.

"I'll talk to her," Holly promised.

"Thank you, my dear. You're a true hero."

She was still glowing from the words "true hero" as she hopped up the stairs. Outside Periwinkle's room, she steadied herself and took a deep breath.

She poked her nose in. "Periwinkle?"

Inside the room, the ribbons seemed to have multiplied — they were everywhere, from ceiling to wall. Many of them were braided, and pebbles decorated the floor in an even more elaborate pattern than Holly had chosen. *Periwinkle has been busy.* She thought it was a good sign that Periwinkle had kept the room neat on her own. She ducked under a purple satin ribbon. "Where did you find all of these?"

Periwinkle's voice drifted from somewhere deep within the web of ribbons. "They're mine."

"I believe you." She knew that none of the other creatures kept ribbons. Maybe Periwinkle had found them at nearby farms? There were a few human households within a five-mile radius of the shelter. Holly examined one of the ribbons. It was made from frayed fabric. The lemur could have been finding lost pieces of human clothes and then tearing them into strips to decorate her room.

"Because all the items were lost," Periwinkle continued, "and — what?"

Holly repeated, "I believe you."

"Oh. Okay."

"I'm back from my adventure," Holly said. She paused for a moment, savoring that word. It *had* been an adventure. "How have you been?"

The lemur was silent for a moment. "Fine."

"Are the others being nice to you?" She couldn't imagine that Charlie had been anything but nice. But she also couldn't guess what else had happened. Last time she'd talked with Periwinkle, she'd thought they'd made progress.

"Yes."

"That's good." Holly settled down on a pile of ribbons. She played with the fur on her tail, brushing it flat with her paw. "So, why are you hiding from everyone?"

"I'm not."

She caught a glimpse of movement in the ribbons but pretended she didn't. She continued to focus on her tail. She'd gotten sand in her fur. Shaking it out, she said, "Do you want to tell me why you refused to help Charlie?"

"No."

"Okay," Holly said. She was careful not to sound judgmental.

Digging her paw deeper into her tail, she plucked out more grains of sand.

"You're not going to insist I explain myself?" Periwinkle emerged from the ribbons a few feet from Holly and sat on her haunches. Her striped tail was raised up behind her, alert.

"Do you want to explain yourself?"

"No."

"Then I won't insist." Holly felt the lemur watching her, and she continued to root out more sand as she waited for the lemur's next move.

The lemur crept nearer. "What is in your fur?"

"Sand," Holly said. "We went to the ocean."

Coming even closer, the lemur plucked a grain of sand from Holly's back fur. "I've never seen the ocean." She found another grain near Holly's left ear. She flicked it across the room.

Holly described what she'd seen and what had happened as Periwinkle helped groom her fur. She didn't talk about the spell ingredients that Charlie wanted help with, and she didn't ask any more questions about the ribbons. Instead she told her about flying with Gus, about Zephyr and Leaf stuck on the rock, and about talking with Cerulean while Gus and Leaf flew Zephyr to shore.

When she finished, Periwinkle said, "You're lucky to have a friend like Gus."

"I am," Holly agreed.

"I've never had a friend."

"You have one," Holly said. "Me. And you could have more,

if you want them. But you can't just push everyone away and then wonder why they aren't friendlier."

Periwinkle stared at her.

Holly took a deep breath and pressed on. "You know we need all seven ingredients to cast the spell. Charlie says he needs your help to find the last two, but he said you refused."

"If I say I'll do it, and then I can't, everyone's going to hate me."

Holly knew no one would hold failure against Periwinkle — much less "hate" her for it. All the shelterlings had failed before, after all. Holly was sure they'd understand . . . though they would be disappointed. Maybe Periwinkle sensed that.

She's afraid, Holly thought. She could understand that, especially since the lemur had faced judgmental treatment before. "Why do you think you'll fail? You found all of this!" Holly waved her paw at all the ribbons and pebbles.

"What if I get wherever Charlie says to go, and I can't see a glow? What if I can't find it and it just stays lost?"

"If you don't at least try, it's certain to stay lost."

Periwinkle's eyes widened even more than usual. "Do you think . . . if I come out of my room and try to help the beaver find what he wants . . . will it show the others I can be friendly?"

"I think it would be a good start," Holly said.

Chapter Twelve

As Holly coaxed Periwinkle downstairs, she called, "Charlie? Periwinkle's ready!"

The beaver hurried into the foyer with his satchel slung over his shoulder. "Excellent! If we're quick, we can make it to the fallen star today. But we have to leave now."

"Right now?" Periwinkle asked. "Why?"

Ignoring her question, Charlie clapped his paw on the lemur's back and said, "Welcome to your first quest, Periwinkle! And well done, Holly!" He bellowed as if he were inviting everyone in the shelter to a party. "Come see us off! We've got a train to catch!"

"You're taking a train?" Holly asked, surprised. Animals didn't ride trains. Or maybe familiars did. But certainly not anyone Holly knew.

"Come with us." Periwinkle snagged Holly's paw in hers.

"That's not necessary," Charlie said.

Holly agreed. It was unlikely that pastry powers would be useful in finding a fallen star. "You can do this, Periwinkle. I've seen your power in action. Remember when you found the clothespin? And Bluebell's hat?"

Entering the foyer, Bluebell sniffed loudly. Curious, other shelterlings appeared — emerging from the warren beneath the farmhouse, as well as coming out of their rooms upstairs.

Squeezing Holly's paw, Periwinkle said, "Please come, Holly?"

She heard the anxiousness in Periwinkle's "please." *I'm right that it's fear*, Holly thought. *That's why she pushes away others, rejecting them before they can reject her. And that's why she wants me to come: she trusts me.* "Charlie only needs you . . ."

Loudly, to Charlie, Periwinkle proclaimed, "I won't go without my friend."

Charlie studied the lemur, with his furry face squished into a frown. It occurred to Holly that he didn't understand Periwinkle. He was used to being adored. Periwinkle was used to being pushed away or dismissed. It was entirely possible that Holly was the first creature who had tried to understand *why* Periwinkle acted the way she did.

"Holly has traveled a lot already," Charlie said. "I wouldn't want to ask too much of —"

A train whistle blew.

"Holly . . ." Periwinkle pleaded.

Holly chirped, "I'll come!"

If Charlie was surprised, he covered it well. He sounded so boisterous that it nearly seemed as if it had been his idea in the first place. "Excellent! Then we three are off!"

They were swept out the door with the other excited shelterlings.

Holly glanced up at the eaves, where Gus still slept. "Wait, I need to tell Gus —"

"There's no more time for delay, my dear," Charlie said. "You heard the whistle. The train runs on a schedule. If you wish to come, we must be at the stop to meet it."

"Gus!" she called. "Wake up! I'm going on a trip!"

But Gus slept on.

Maybe there was time to run up the side of the house and shake him awake . . . But Charlie was already striding toward the trellis. "Bluebell," Holly called, "when Gus wakes, will you tell him where I've gone? Tell him I'm going on another adventure, and I'll be back soon."

Doffing his hat, the rabbit bowed. "I will, brave squirrel."

Holly laughed and then scampered after Charlie and Periwinkle. A new adventure! And a chance to ride a train! *Gus will understand*, she thought.

Reaching the trellis, Charlie halted. "Periwinkle?" Rising up on his hind legs, he looked for her across the lawn. Several shelterlings had gathered around her. He called, "Come on, my dear! Hurry!"

The other animals parted, and for an instant, Holly thought Periwinkle was going to bolt, but she didn't. As she tentatively walked toward Charlie, the others began to speak up: "Good luck, Periwinkle." "Thanks, Periwinkle." "Good luck."

As the chorus of well-wishes grew, Periwinkle walked with more confidence.

Leaving the yard, the three of them set off together across the field. The sun warmed Holly's fur, and she ran ahead through the grass. She'd often heard the train chug past, but she'd never thought she'd be boarding it. Behind her, Charlie and Periwinkle were talking — the lemur asking questions, the beaver answering — but Holly didn't listen. She was busy wondering what it would be like to ride a train.

She didn't think it would be like flying, but the train did travel much faster than any squirrel could. She wondered if it would feel like being transported within the belly of a beast. She imagined it would be loud inside, with everything rumbling all around, and she tried to guess whether it would be frightening or marvelous. It would certainly be new.

She'd lost count of how many new experiences she'd had since Charlie had returned. She used to just dream about new experiences, and now here she was!

Reaching the tracks, Holly halted as her paws hit gravel. In front of her lay the iron rails, thick and heavy with ties like tree trunks between them. She sniffed the air and smelled metal, as well as the lingering hint of smoke from all the other times the train had puffed past.

Nearby, she spotted a wood hut only a few feet from the tracks. She'd never thought to wonder what the hut was for. It didn't look like anyone lived there. Why was it so close to the tracks? How were they supposed to board the train? How were the other passengers going to react to the shelterlings? She had so many questions!

Holly waited impatiently for the others to catch up. As soon as they reached her, she ran in a circle around Charlie. "How do we do it?" she asked. "How do we ride the train?"

"See how the tracks pass that shack?" Charlie said. "The train always stops there for a mail pickup. So we'll just jump on with the mail."

"You've done this before?" Holly asked.

"Lots of times."

"No one minds?" Periwinkle asked.

"Nah," Charlie said. "They'll think we're familiars on our way to join our wizards. If you ride the train with purpose, the humans will assume you're supposed to be there. They don't care. Everyone's busy with their own business; they can't be bothered with yours. Come on. It'll be here soon." He hurried toward the shack, and Holly and Periwinkle followed.

Climbing onto the roof of the mail shack, Holly watched for the train.

Both Charlie and Periwinkle stayed on the ground, which was fine by Holly. She wanted to think about what Charlie had said — that no one cared, or could even tell, if she was a familiar or not. She'd never imagined that was a possibility.

Closer this time, Holly heard the train whistle.

"It's coming!" she called down to Charlie and Periwinkle.

She caught a glimpse of the train's smoke curling above the trees. The whistle blew again. Rising up on her hind paws, Holly watched the train chug out of the forest and along the track toward them. She admired its sleek silver paint, the tall smokestack, and the triangular grille that looked like a mouth. She'd never seen a train so close before. As it slowed, Holly felt her heart beat faster and faster.

Grinding to a halt with a loud squeal, the train stopped in front of the mail shack, and a conductor in a blue-and-silver suit opened the door to one of the cars. She stomped out and proceeded to load burlap sacks from within the shack onto the train.

"Good day," Charlie said to her.

"Good day," the conductor replied in a brisk voice. "Don't make a mess, and you can sit in any open compartment. Ticketed passengers get priority for seats."

"Understood," Charlie said politely. "Thank you."

And that was it. No questions about where they were going, why they weren't with a wizard, or why they thought they had the right to travel like proper familiars. Charlie shooed Periwinkle onto the train, and Holly jumped from the roof onto the steps of the train car.

Maybe Charlie's right, Holly thought. *Maybe no one cares if we're familiars or not.*

Charlie led them to a set of seats with red upholstery. Four full-size humans could have sat in them, but they were empty. Holly marveled at it.

Periwinkle huddled in her seat and clutched her ringed tail to her chest.

"It'll be okay," Holly told her, though she'd never been on a train either. But she trusted Charlie, and he climbed onto his seat and settled in as if he'd done this hundreds of times.

The train lurched into motion. As it chugged faster, Holly

pressed herself against the dust-streaked window and watched the blur of scenery: fields and orchards, meadows and hills, then forests. The light shifted from bright to dark as they traveled beneath tree branches. She hadn't expected a light show!

Still curled into a ball, Periwinkle asked, "Where are we going?"

"I was able to learn the location of a crater," Charlie said. "It's a few years old and small, but locals still talk about it, which was how I heard of it."

"What's a crater?" Periwinkle asked.

"When bits of rocks from beyond the sky fall to earth, they fall so hard they make holes in the ground called craters. I believe that's where our predecessors found their 'fallen star.' We need to find a chunk of meteorite for our spell."

"If you know where it is, why do you need me? I thought you needed my special power to find a lost item."

Holly was wondering that same thing.

"The trick is that space rock doesn't look any different from ordinary rock, at least not to me," Charlie said. "I need you to find specks of rock lost from the sky and separate them from the specks of ordinary dirt that belong here."

Periwinkle bobbed her head enthusiastically. "Lost things glow for me, and then I can find them! Want to see?"

Before he could answer, she darted off her seat and disappeared deeper into the train car. She returned after a minute with a button in her paw. Showing it to Charlie and Holly, she dropped it onto a seat cushion and departed again.

"Should we stop her?" Charlie asked.

"She's practicing," Holly said. "It's good for her." *And she wants to make certain she won't fail,* Holly thought.

Periwinkle continued to dart back and forth, each time bringing back a new stray item, and Holly returned to gawking out the window.

Eventually, the train slowed and then squealed to a halt.

"Is this our stop?" Periwinkle asked.

"Indeed it is," Charlie said.

"Ready!" The lemur tried to lift a shoe overflowing with lost items. A necklace slithered out and slipped to coil snakelike on the floor. She struggled to balance the rest against her thigh.

"You may want to leave those here," Charlie said. His voice was gentle, but Holly watched Periwinkle to see how she'd respond.

"Why? They're mine!"

"Of course they are," Holly quickly jumped in. "But what Charlie means is that we'll have enough to carry once we find the space rocks. That's why we're here, remember?"

Charlie added, "Everyone's going to be so happy if we come back with the sixth ingredient. We'll only be one step away from casting the spell!"

With a wistful look at her stash, Periwinkle left it on the train seat, and Holly wanted to cheer. She'd thought that was going to turn into an argument. Apparently, Periwinkle wanted approval even more than she wanted her lost things.

Trailing after Charlie and Periwinkle to the exit, Holly saw the lemur dart under another seat just before the door. She snagged a scarf from beneath the seat and wrapped it around her neck.

They followed Charlie as he waddled off the train.

Noticing the scarf, he said, "Space rocks, not scarves."

Looking downcast, Periwinkle unwound the scarf and held it in her paws.

"It's not too much to carry," Holly told her. "And you look lovely in it." She shot Charlie a glance, but he didn't contradict her.

Giving Holly a grateful look, the lemur wrapped it back around her neck.

"Come," Charlie said. "Our prize awaits."

✦

The crater lay before them, a weed-choked bowl in the center of a pasture. A few sheep grazed on the opposite side, ignoring the beaver, lemur, and squirrel. It didn't, Holly thought, look like anything special. She'd expected a hole caused by a falling star to be a bit more, well, starlike. As Charlie had said, it was impossible to tell what was space debris and what was ordinary dirt — it all looked the same.

"My dear, it's your turn to shine," Charlie said to Periwinkle. "Find us the lost bit of star, and you will be the hero of us all!"

"I can do it!" she cried as she ran down the side of the crater into the bowl.

Holly and Charlie watched her scamper through the grass in an excited zigzag. "You've really done wonders with her," Charlie said.

"All I did was talk to her," Holly said. "She's the one who chose to help. I think she wants to be one of us. She just hasn't known how."

On the floor of the crater, the lemur jumped up and down. Holding a chunk of rock in the air, Periwinkle waved it back and forth.

Pride in his voice, Charlie said, "Well, she's proved herself now."

Excited, Holly waved her tail at Periwinkle. "She did that fast!"

With her prize, Periwinkle hurried across the crater. She climbed up the slope and presented the rock with both hands.

And Holly saw that it wasn't a rock at all. It was a twisted bit of metal. She could smell the remnants of oil and the tangy scent of rust.

Leaning forward, Charlie sniffed it. "Periwinkle, that's a tractor part."

"I know, but it's so nice and shiny that I thought you'd like it too."

"Not a space rock," Holly said gently. "Try again?"

Periwinkle dropped the tractor part on the grass and scampered back down into the crater. Both Holly and Charlie watched her intently without talking this time. She crisscrossed the dirt and tall grass again.

Stopping, she lifted another item aloft: a boot.

After they both shook their heads, she tossed it away and continued searching. Sighing, Holly sat back on her haunches. She wished she could help, but a nose for acorns wasn't useful in finding meteorites. They had to trust in Periwinkle's power.

After several minutes (and many more random objects), Periwinkle returned to the lip of the crater. "I'm sorry," she said. "I can't find it."

"You have to keep trying," Charlie said.

She shook her head. "I don't know if rock can be lost. It's rock. It doesn't really belong to anyone." She waved the tip of her scarf in the air. "Unlike this. It once belonged to someone, but they didn't appreciate it enough to keep track of it. So it became lost, and I could find it. Bits of rock from outer space, though . . ."

"We need the meteorite. The spell won't work without it." Charlie took his satchel off and gave it to Periwinkle. "There should be lots of chunks of space rock in the crater. Gather up every bit you find."

"But I haven't found any!"

Holly said encouragingly, "Keep trying. Your power is amazing!"

Sighing, Periwinkle tied off the satchel strap to shorten it, then put it over her shoulder. It still dragged on the ground. "It's not as if I *want* to fail. I know this is important. I just can't find something that isn't actually lost."

"You found Bluebell's hat," Holly said. "He wouldn't have called it lost, but you still found it. Your magic is powerful. We just have to find a way to guide it. Like Clover and her rhymes." She'd coached other shelterlings on how to fine-tune their magic. Surely she could help Periwinkle now.

"But how?"

Holly took Periwinkle's paws and turned her to face the crater. She tried to think of this as just another practice session with Clover or Tangerine. It was better if she didn't focus on how important it was that Periwinkle succeed. She kept her voice calm and upbeat. "Somewhere in those weeds are pieces of rock that aren't from here."

"That's not the same as lost."

"It kind of is," Holly said. "The rock is not where anyone expects it to be. And no one else appreciates that it's here. Look at how ignored the crater is." The sheep milled around it as if it were nothing. There were no tracks. No sign that anyone cared it was here.

Periwinkle blinked. "You're right."

"Think of the meteorite as lost." She didn't know if that was enough to activate Periwinkle's power, but she was betting that neither did Periwinkle. They wouldn't know until they tried. "Concentrate on that idea: lost space rock. It's not where it belongs, and as much as we want to find it, it's lost to us."

Periwinkle opened her mouth and then closed it, thinking. Letting go of Holly's paws, Periwinkle focused on the crater, her tail held at alert.

Holly held her breath.

Suddenly, Periwinkle danced from paw to paw. "I see a new glow! Lots of new glows!"

"Good job!" Charlie said.

With Charlie's satchel slung over her shoulder, Periwinkle scampered down into the crater and began sniffing through the weeds.

Chirping with delight, she zipped back and forth. She scooped up what looked like rocks and shoved them into the satchel.

She's doing it! Holly thought.

Charlie patted Holly on the shoulder. "Good job to you, too."

All the lemur had needed was someone to believe in her. And maybe to help her see things a little differently. She was doing the rest herself.

Periwinkle stuck her paw into the weeds —

"Ow!" She snatched her paw back and cradled it to her chest.

"Periwinkle!" Holly scurried into the crater. In half a minute, she'd reached the lemur. "Are you all right? What happened?"

"Something bit me!" Nursing her paw, Periwinkle glared at the weeds as she retreated.

Peeling open her fingers, Holly examined her palm. There were two indents with red dots. The lemur had clearly been bitten, but who —

A rat poked its head out from between the weeds. "Give us everything you have."

Holly chittered at him. "You bit her! That was rude!"

The rat didn't care. "We saw you come on the train. We followed you here. You're clearly seeking treasure and wouldn't have made such an effort if what you wanted weren't valuable. Now give us your bag."

"Us?" Holly asked.

"Holly, another one!" Periwinkle cried.

A second rat had emerged from behind them and was gnawing at the satchel strap. "Mine," it said between mouthfuls.

"It's not," Periwinkle said. She had some of her old attitude back — this time, Holly thought, it was completely appropriate. "It's ours!"

"Yeah, but can you keep it?" the first rat taunted. He made a shrill squeal, and three more rats spilled into the crater. Startled, the nearby sheep shied away.

Five rats closed in on Holly and Periwinkle. Shrieking, Periwinkle dropped the satchel and ran back across the crater toward Charlie. The rats swarmed over the bag.

"Stop that!" Holly said. "That's not yours! Why are you doing this?"

One of the rats — a muscular one with bald patches of fur — said, "It's what we do. See what looks good, and then we take it."

Another shrugged. "We're rats. We have to live up to our reputation."

"No, you don't," Holly said. "You don't have to do this at all."

"All right, then," the large rat said. "We don't *have* to do this." He paused. "We *want* to do this."

The other rats cackled.

Maybe she could tempt them away from the satchel with a pastry. Concentrating, she conjured an éclair and tossed it toward the rats. "You can have this, if you leave us the bag and the rocks."

A smaller rat sniffed at an éclair, and for a second, Holly thought it was going to work. She would negotiate, the way she had with the dragon and the orca . . . But before she could try, Charlie bellowed, "Let that go, you vermin!"

The rats surrounded the satchel. Snarling and baring their

fangs, all of them were larger than Holly. She shuddered to the tip of her tail and then fled.

"What are you doing, Holly?" Charlie cried. "We need that bag!"

Sides heaving, Holly looked down into the bowl. The rats were swarming over Charlie's satchel, gnawing at the canvas. "I think it's theirs now." Every muscle felt tense. What if the rats tired of the satchel and turned on them? They three of them were outnumbered. "If we talk to them, maybe we can find a way to compromise —"

Charlie cut her off. "No. All my notes are in there. All my research, as well as the spell itself. Not to mention the sixth ingredient. Without that bag, everything will be ruined!"

"I'll get it back," Periwinkle promised.

Brave Periwinkle, Holly thought, with a burst of pride.

"But I don't know how," she admitted.

Down in the crater, the five rats were snapping at one another as they tugged the satchel toward the opposite side of the bowl. Holly didn't see a way for the lemur to reach it. Five rats! Even Charlie, as large as he was, couldn't fight off five rats without risking being bitten worse than Periwinkle had been. "It's not safe for her to go into the crater. The rats —"

"I will take care of the rats." He bit off each word as he glared down into the crater.

Holly's whiskers twitched. She'd never heard him sound like that. Vicious. Dangerous.

"Grab the satchel, Periwinkle, as soon as the rats are distracted," he said. "We lost it, so it should glow for you. You'll be able to see it regardless of what's going on around you."

What did he mean, *what's going on around you?* Before Holly could ask, Charlie stepped to the edge of the crater.

He waved his arms in the air, and flowers began to spill out of his open paws. He waded through the crater with more and more blooms flowing out of him.

Roses.

Holly recognized them from the shelter gardens. Red, white, pink . . . they tumbled from his paws faster and faster. Piling on top of one another, they mounded on the crater's floor.

Periwinkle darted down the slope toward the roses. She aimed for the center of the crater as the rats tried to swim through the ever-growing pile of roses. Holly heard the rats squeal in confusion and pain.

As the flowers piled higher, she saw glimpses of the lemur scurrying through the roses and between the rats. And then Holly lost sight of Periwinkle entirely as the cascade of roses blocked her view. Periwinkle was somewhere in there, with the rats. Holly hoped she was okay, that she had the satchel, that she could find her way out. She held her breath. *Come on, Periwinkle,* she thought. *You can do this. I know you can!*

Suddenly, Periwinkle popped out of the roses. She flopped onto the grass, with the satchel lying over her belly. "Charlie?" she called. "You can stop now."

Holly ran to the lemur. "Are you all right?"

"I'm fine, but . . . is he okay?" She pointed a paw at the beaver.

On the side of the crater, Charlie was standing on his hind legs. He was conjuring and tossing rose after rose into the crater in rapid succession.

Holly crossed to him and tentatively laid a paw on his arm. "Charlie?"

He turned on her, and she saw that his muzzle was twisted in rage, teeth exposed and gums curled back. Holly shrank away. He barely looked like her old friend at all.

He snapped out a question: "Did she get it?"

Joining them, Periwinkle gave him the bag. "You lost this. I found it."

At the sight of it, he seemed to deflate, all his rage draining out of him. He hugged the satchel to his chest. "Miraculous," he praised her.

Periwinkle beamed, which Holly thought was a lovely moment and all, but the rats were still out there. "Can we go?" Holly asked. "Before the rats regroup and come after us?"

All three of them hurried away from the crater, with Charlie's satchel and the precious bits of fallen star.

CHAPTER THIRTEEN

On the train home, Holly wrapped Periwinkle's paw in her new scarf. "You'll be fine," she told her. She'd helped the lemur clean out the wound in the train bathroom, and the very nice train conductor had given them an ointment to prevent infection. She hadn't asked if they were familiars or not, which continued to feel wondrous to Holly. Now they were back in their seats. "Just keep the cuts clean, and they'll heal up on their own."

Periwinkle flexed her paw within the scarf. "It doesn't hurt anymore."

"Good," Holly said. "You were really brave in the crater."

"Never been called 'brave' before, and I've been called a lot of things. Usually 'annoying.' Or worse."

"You did well," Charlie told the lemur kindly.

Curling up in her seat, Periwinkle rested her head on the cushion. She looked happy, Holly thought. Holly met Charlie's eyes, and he gave her an approving nod.

As the train chugged across the countryside, Periwinkle drifted to sleep while Charlie studied his notebook. Holly guessed he was thinking about the final ingredient. She knew that she was. Just one more! They were so close!

Looking out the train window, she imagined what it would feel like to be at the Moon Mirror again but this time with all her friends around her. She pictured them, side by side, drinking from the water all at the same time. She'd been alone at the pool before. It would feel so different — so much better — this time. She loved that thought.

As they passed a farm with a field of horses, she heard a snort-like snore in addition to the lemur's soft wheeze, and glanced back to see that Charlie was scooched down with his broad tail behind him like a pillow. Holly still felt too jittery and excited to sleep.

I wish I could have helped more, Holly thought. But at least she'd cheered on Periwinkle and helped her focus her magic. The lemur had been able to control it better, once Holly had redefined what it meant for an item to be "lost." That would be useful when they went to look for the crystal.

As Charlie slept, the notebook slipped from his paw and thumped to the floor.

Holly climbed off the seat to pick it up. Certainly he wouldn't want to lose that! Of course, Periwinkle could find it again if he did, but still . . .

Pushing and pulling the notebook, she climbed back up onto the seat next to Charlie. She plopped onto the cushion with the notebook beside her and panted. It wasn't a large book — at least not in comparison to the ones she'd seen wizards carrying at the

Wizards Tower — but it was still significantly larger than an acorn, and the climb had been awkward. Worth it, though. He'd recorded all his notes about the ingredients in these pages.

Ooh, maybe he'd written something that could help them find the last ingredient — a clue he'd forgotten or overlooked! She thought about how happy he'd be if, when he woke, she could tell him she knew exactly where Periwinkle should look for the crystal.

Flipping through the pages, she saw he'd filled every inch of space with details of his search for the spell, as well as his research on what the ingredients were and where to find them. There was page after page of notes in his cramped handwriting. She studied them, fascinated. She felt his joy radiating off the pages where he wrote about the moment he, at long last, had discovered the details of the spell, especially the key fact that it was cast with seven magic items. It almost felt like being there herself. She marveled at his persistence and his patience, which were paying off at last. He really had been, as he'd said, chasing the truth.

She turned the page and there it was, in crisp ink, written in formal script as if it had been copied from a book: the spell itself. It was written in glyphs, the language of spells.

With the help of their familiars, wizards used glyphs to work magic. The wizard either carved them on objects, like the rocks in the arrival circle, to be activated by touch, or spoke the spell out loud with the familiar to cast it immediately.

This spell was *the* spell, the one that the long-ago group of animals had cast on the pool at the top of Cloud Mountain. She touched the glyphs reverently with a claw. She knew how to pronounce the glyphs, and she even recognized a few of them, but most were far more advanced than any she'd learned. Only wizards and familiars were fluent enough in the ancient language of magic to understand advanced spells. And this was certainly advanced. In fact, it was the most complex bit of magic she'd ever seen.

On the back of the page, Charlie had written a second copy of the spell. Except it didn't look exactly the same . . . She compared the two — they were identical in parts, but in some areas, Charlie had added new glyphs and altered others. She wondered what these changes meant. Were they improvements, or were they corrections?

He'd done so much and worked so hard. He'd learned the language of wizardry, studied the glyphs, and chased down bits of history that had been lost to myth and legend. *And he did it all alone,* Holly thought. *If we'd known* . . . The shelterlings would have helped him sooner, if he'd asked. She was glad they were able to help now. Gently, she touched one of the glyphs, trying to imagine what Charlie had been thinking and feeling when he wrote it —

"What are you doing?" Charlie cried. He ripped the notebook out of her paws.

Across the aisle, Periwinkle blinked awake, clearly confused. She frowned at the book, open to Charlie's altered spell. "What is that?"

Charlie snapped the notebook shut.

"I was —" Holly tried to explain. She shrank back from the raw fury on his face. His muzzle was curled into a snarl, revealing two pairs of teeth strong enough to chew down trees.

"This is private!"

"I'm sorry, Charlie. I was just —"

"Well, you shouldn't have!" he yelled, with a glare that could have melted an iceberg. His teeth were still bared.

Periwinkle jumped across the train car and positioned herself in front of Holly. "Why are you yelling at Holly? Don't yell at Holly!"

With a snarl, Charlie shoved the battered notebook deep into the satchel, and a space rock spilled out. Periwinkle scurried over the seat to collect it. She held it out to Charlie.

Taking a breath to calm himself, he accepted the meteorite. He forced his expression to soften. "Thank you, Periwinkle. Holly, I apologize for yelling."

"And I'm sorry for looking at your notebook." Holly had never seen him react like that. Charlie had always been the friendliest, calmest, most affable creature she'd ever met. If she'd been asked if he had a temper, she would have said no, nothing could ruffle his fur.

Except for rats trying to steal his satchel, she thought. *And me looking at his notebook.*

Periwinkle pivoted between them, looking at Charlie, then at Holly, then back at Charlie. When there was no more yelling, she settled back into her seat.

Charlie reached over and patted Holly on her head. "All's well. I am just on edge because I don't know where to begin looking for the final ingredient. It's all that stands between us and success."

"We'll help," Periwinkle said.

"All we want to do is help," Holly said. "That's what I was trying to do."

"Of course. I know that."

They didn't speak of it again for the rest of the journey. Charlie kept the satchel with the notebook close to him, both paws wrapped around it, and Holly sat in the uneasy silence, trying not to wonder why he hadn't wanted her to see what he'd written.

✦

After they disembarked from the train, it was only a short run back across the field to the shelter. Scampering through the grass, Holly ran faster and faster until she burst through the trellis. She wasn't certain if she was running *to* the shelter or *from* her worries about Charlie and his notebook, and she didn't want to examine that question too closely.

"Gus!" she called. "Gus, I'm back!"

Above her, Gus soared out the second-story window, and Holly ran in a circle beneath him, hoping he wasn't upset. She didn't think she could handle both Gus and Charlie, her two dearest friends, being unhappy with her at the same time.

He glided down to the lawn to land next to her.

"I'm sorry I didn't wake you," she said immediately.

"I'm sorry I didn't wake up," he said at exactly the same time.

Both of them laughed. She felt one worry melt away. He wasn't mad at her, and that was a wonderful thing.

"Now that that's settled," Gus said, "tell me everything!"

"The most important thing is that we have the meteorite," Holly said. "So that leaves only one ingredient." She felt like crowing as she said it. Only one left! "Getting it wasn't easy, though. There were these rats . . ." She told him about the five belligerent rats who'd tried to steal Charlie's satchel and about how Charlie had fought back with roses. "But, thanks to Periwinkle, we made it to the train with the satchel and without the rats."

"You rode on a train?" he asked.

"No one seemed to mind," Holly said. "In fact, they barely noticed." As Charlie had predicted, no one had cared whether they were familiars or not. None of the other passengers had so much as glanced at them, either on the way there or on the way back. Everyone had gone about their own business and not had any interest in who the animals were or why they were there. "It felt . . . I can't describe it . . . I felt like I could go anywhere I wanted to on that train, and the only thing that might stop me was, well, me."

Poking his head out the door, Bluebell called, "They've returned! More stanzas for my ballad! Huzzah!" He hopped outside, followed by other shelterlings. Everyone gathered around Holly, wanting to know where they'd gone, what had happened, and, most important, had they found the fallen star?

As Periwinkle and Charlie came through the trellis, Holly waved Periwinkle over. "Periwinkle was the hero," she told the other shelterlings. "She found the meteorite, and she won it for us against a gang of rats."

"Rats?" Tangerine shuddered, his quills changing color. "Nasty creatures."

Holly couldn't deny that, in this case. She described for a second time what had happened, warming to her story, adding more details (and rats) and gesturing with her paws and tail.

With appreciative murmurs and gasps in all the appropriate places, the others crowded around Periwinkle. The little lemur looked tense at first, and then relaxed as she realized they were congratulating her.

Holly watched, pleased. The lemur deserved the praise.

At Charlie's suggestion, they brought the spell ingredients to the living room and set them out on the floor: the pearl, the volcanic rock, the desert fruit, the herb, and the meteorite.

Drawn by the commotion, more shelterlings poured into the living room. Greeting them, Charlie picked up the largest chunk of meteorite in his paw and held it high. "My friends, we're almost there! Look, we've found the star rock!"

"Wow! Is it really from space?" Zephyr asked.

"Here, you can touch it," Charlie said. Magnanimously, he passed the meteorite around. "Go on, everyone, this is a moment to celebrate." Oohing and aahing, the shelterlings passed it from claw to claw, beak to beak.

While everyone admired the fallen star, Holly fetched the wilting magic flower to show Charlie. He waved his paw over it, and the stem straightened, the petals perked up, and the magic glow strengthened. Holly gasped. "I didn't know you could do that!"

He shrugged. "A parlor trick."

"Bringing plants back to life isn't a minor trick!" She wondered if he'd experimented on dead plants. How about seeds? Could he grow plants from seeds? She thought of his notebook, and she wondered if he'd ever done any research into his own power. She could help him with that, if he wanted.

"My power is merely decorative," Charlie said. "It only works with cut flowers."

She remembered how he'd filled the crater with roses to stop the rats and thought that Charlie was underselling himself, but he'd already moved on to the next topic. Addressing everyone, he said, "You've done well, my friends, but the last item we need is the most elusive. I've learned from my research that we seek a crystal, hidden within a cave. It's my hope that once we're close enough, 'hidden' will be sufficiently similar to 'lost' that our dear Periwinkle can find it."

"I can," the lemur said confidently.

"However, we need to know where to begin our search."

"And how will we determine that?" Bluebell asked. He was wearing a bonnet covered in flowers, in Charlie's honor, though his flowers were made of silk.

Charlie sighed heavily. "I had hoped to be much further along in solving this mystery by now."

One of the mice jumped up and down. "Can we help?"

Others chimed in: they wanted to help too. Maybe they could go on a quest to uncover where to go on the quest. One suggested they visit libraries. Another said they should consult the wise. A few decided this obstacle was a sign that the whole endeavor was doomed. Leaf said he should have known this wouldn't work. Pepper agreed, saying she'd been a fool to get her hopes up. But others argued back, shouting out ideas that were a mix of practical and absurd.

As the other shelterlings chattered and argued and shouted suggestions, Holly saw Gus glide out the window. Following him, she hopped up onto the sill. Why was he —

She saw him fly into the barn.

Clover! she thought.

"Brilliant, Gus," Holly whispered. The cow had the potential to be tremendously helpful, if she could just get her magic to cooperate. It wasn't easy. When she tried to predict the weather, she'd spout a prophecy about the lettuce crop. But Holly and Gus had been working with her to fine-tune her power.

Maybe she'd have enough control to help them find the crystal.

Holly scurried out the window and scampered across the lawn toward the barn. As she entered, she heard voices: Gus and Clover. He was filling her in on their situation.

The barn was cavernous, with rafters high above. Sunlight flooded in through open windows, and dust sparkled in the air. The floor was covered in a thick mat of hay. Thanks to Strawberry the skunk and her power over odors, it smelled like flowers instead of manure. Holly passed several stalls before she reached Clover's.

Gus was perched on the side of the stall, and Clover was chewing on hay. Stalks drooped out of her mouth as she chewed and listened. Holly waved her tail in the air. "Gus, did you ask her? Clover, can you do it? Can you divine the location of the magic crystal?"

"He asked me," Clover said. "But . . ."

"Would you please try? For us?"

Clover shifted from hoof to hoof as she looked at Holly and Gus. "My, oh my, for you of course I'll try, but I can't promise it will work. You know my predictions tend to be . . . unpredictable."

"We'll help you," Holly said. "Remember what we were practicing with the rhymes?"

"I know, but my degree of accuracy . . . is not always what I'd like it to be."

The cow was reliably wrong, which wasn't a problem as long as you knew that. "Let us worry about accuracy," Holly said.

Clover looked back and forth between Holly and Gus, who nodded encouragingly. She cleared her throat and intoned: "On tomorrow's morn, the rain will fall, so hard that even the fish will bawl." She then made a face. "Oh, another weather one."

"That's okay," Holly said supportively. "You're just getting warmed up."

Clover tried again: "The train will be late on an unspecified date."

"Excellent rhyme," Gus cheered. "Try to rhyme the word 'crystal.'"

Clover stared into the empty space above Gus's head. "Crystal . . . find the crystal . . ." she said. After a long moment, she sighed. "Nothing's coming. Usually knowledge just appears in my head all shiny, and that's what I need to talk about."

"Did you say 'shiny'?" Periwinkle asked from above them.

Holly looked up and saw the lemur walking along the rafters. "Periwinkle?"

Periwinkle leaped from one rafter to another and then climbed down toward Clover's stall. "I followed you," she said to Holly. To Clover she said, "You mean your prophecies glow in your head?"

"Yes, 'glow' is an excellent way to describe it. The words glow. How did you know?"

"Lost things glow for me. But I need to be paying attention and looking in the right direction. Maybe it's the same with you? Maybe you need to . . . well, 'look' in the right direction."

Holly watched Clover to see if that helped.

"But I already tried thinking about the crystal," Clover said.

Gus cocked his head, thinking. "Were you, though? Or were you thinking about how much we all want you to find it?"

"Try closing your eyes so you're not looking at us," Holly suggested.

Clover obeyed.

"I'm going to say some words," Holly said. "Stop me when one glows. 'Crystal.' 'Magic.' 'Hidden.'"

Clover quit chewing her cud. "'Hidden' . . . Yes!"

They all held their breath.

At last the cow intoned, "The crystal that you seek will not be found within a peak. It lies in a . . . um, I need a rhyme."

"Leak, sneak, reek," Gus said.

"Meek, beak," Holly added.

"Freak?" Periwinkle suggested.

Clover finished. "It lies within a beak!"

"It's within a mountain, everyone," Gus translated. "Good job, Clover. We know it's in a cave, so that makes sense. Lots of mountains have caves."

"Great," Holly said. "Let's try to be more specific. Peak. What peak?"

The cow chewed her cud again. "The peak you seek is not in the . . ." She faltered. "The train will be late on an unspecified date! The rain will fall, the fish will bawl!" Agitated, she shuffled backwards and bumped against the side of the stall.

"North, south, east, or west?" Gus coaxed.

"The peak you seek is not in the . . ." Her eyes popped open. "The peak you seek is not in the east. You shouldn't seek that way in the least!"

So the crystal lay within a cave inside a mountain to the east. Which mountains were to the east? "The Seven Sisters!" Holly said, excitedly. It was a chain of mountains, each one so high its crown was wreathed in snow.

"But which one?" Periwinkle asked.

There were, as the name implied, seven peaks. The three shelterlings looked at Clover.

"Which peak . . . which peak is the one we seek . . . ? Oh! Go to the sister who has never been hungry . . ." Clover looked expectantly at Gus and Holly.

"Uh . . . because she won't eat anything crumbly?" Holly suggested. Gus ruffled his feathers, and she said defensively, "That's not terrible. 'Hungry' is a hard word to rhyme."

"'Sundry' is better," he said.

"I don't know what that word means."

"Neither do I," he admitted. "But it's still a better rhyme."

Periwinkle swished her tail. "You could let her continue."

"Sorry," Holly said. "Please go on, Clover. You're doing great."

Clover looked pleased. "Am I? Really? I thought that last one was a bit cryptic."

"Not at all," Gus said. "We know the crystal is 'not' in a mountain and certainly 'not' to the east. And with your latest line, we know it's 'not' in the Maw."

Holly squinched up her nose. "The what? Oh!" One of the Seven Sisters Mountains was known as the Maw, which meant mouth. Specifically a *hungry* mouth. "That has to be it! You did it, Clover!"

"I did?"

"We need to tell Charlie!" She scampered out of the barn and across the lawn. He was going to be so happy!

Jumping up onto the living-room windowsill, Holly called out, "Charlie! Charlie!" She danced from paw to paw.

He looked up from a conversation with the mice. "Yes, my dear?"

Gus flew in the window and landed on the arm of a chair. Periwinkle joined Holly on the sill. "Charlie," Holly asked, "are there caves in the Maw?"

"Yes, there are. There's a famous cave entrance a third of the way up the mountain. Why do you ask?"

"The crystal — it's there!" Holly beamed at him. "Clover predicted it!"

"Clover?"

Holly waved her tail at Clover as the cow trotted toward the window. Clover should tell them herself. After all, it was her power that was saving the day. She should hear it appreciated.

"As much as I adore her and it pains me to say it," Charlie continued, "Clover is a *cow*. Cows are not . . . how to put this delicately . . . known to be oracles. Clover in particular has never made an accurate or relevant prophecy. I know she wants to help, but —"

Clover stuck her head through the window.

"She's been working hard to improve," Holly said. "Show him, Clover. Tell him where in the Maw to find the crystal. Close your eyes and think *cave*."

Clover closed her eyes.

Coaxing, Holly said, "Up. Down. Right. Left."

"Hush, it's coming . . . I can nearly see the glow . . . Aah . . . First, the path you seek kind of reeks as you go within the peak. Then you must go up, up, up to the very . . . tup?" Clover fluttered open her eyes. "'Top' didn't quite rhyme with 'up.'"

Gus translated. "Follow the path that smells better and then the path that goes down."

"What next?" Holly prompted.

Closing her eyes again, Clover concentrated. "You must head toward the darkest of the dark, if you do not wish to bark."

"We have to head toward the light," Holly translated.

"Do all of this, and the crystal you are sure to miss!"

Periwinkle climbed through the window in the living room. "The crystal will glow for me, once I'm close enough. I'll find it."

Clover opened her eyes and looked hopefully at Holly. "I truly helped?"

Holly glanced at Charlie and saw that he was packing his notebook into his satchel. Zephyr and Pepper were on either side of him, chattering excitedly, and the mice were dancing with the fox.

"You absolutely did," Holly told her.

CHAPTER FOURTEEN

U p on top of the kitchen counter, Holly packed snacks while the others argued in the living room about who would embark on the final quest. Charlie had said he only needed Periwinkle at the Maw, but everyone wanted to help. While they argued and each tried to make their case for why the beaver should pick them to come too, the squirrel sorted through berries and nuts — and she worried.

She kept thinking about the spell. In the glow of having helped Clover succeed, she'd asked Charlie to show the spell to the other shelterlings who were busy handing the ingredients around and congratulating Clover. Holly thought he'd be excited to share his work with everyone, but "Don't be foolish," he'd snapped, and his ice-melting glare returned, then disappeared so fast she almost thought she'd imagined it. Why hadn't Charlie wanted them to see it? She'd understood on the train, sort of, since she hadn't asked first before reading his private notes and thoughts, but why not at least share the finished product? He'd called it private, but it was going to affect all their lives.

Was he was worried it wouldn't work? Was that why he'd added so many glyphs?

What if he didn't understand it as well as he thought he did, or what if he'd made a mistake in his research? What if all his changes made the Moon Mirror worse instead of better? What if it didn't give them the useful magic they all wanted? What if Charlie had made a mistake and was too stubborn or proud to admit it was possible?

Maybe she should have asked him to explain himself, but he'd seemed so upset, and in the moment, she'd just wanted him to stop being upset.

He'd worked hard on the spell, and he clearly believed in it and in himself. She should trust that. *If he says the spell will work, it'll work,* she thought.

As she fetched a napkin, Holly heard paws lightly pad into the kitchen, and the lemur poked her nose over the counter before climbing up to join her.

"I almost have everything ready," Holly said. She tried to sound upbeat. Just because she was worrying didn't mean anyone else needed to worry too. "Only a few more berries to fit in."

"You lost one." Periwinkle held out a blueberry in her paw.

"Oh! Thank you. It must have rolled off the counter. You can eat it, if you want."

Periwinkle nibbled at it, peeling the skin to expose the colorless fruit, while Holly tied the napkin around a pile of berries and nuts. "Holly . . ."

"Yes?"

But the lemur didn't answer.

Holly wondered what was going on inside her mind. Periwinkle looked as if she wanted to ask more questions, but she wasn't saying anything. Cheerfully, Holly said, "You know, I think this is going to work out. We have almost all the items, and we have a good idea of where to search for the last ingredient. Everything is going to be fine."

As she said that, she gave a little shiver. It reminded her of Clover's prophecy on the day that Periwinkle had arrived. She'd said everything would be fine, and then, soon after, both Periwinkle and Charlie had appeared and their quests had begun.

"Holly, will not being a rejected familiar anymore make you happy?"

"Absolutely!" It would be amazing! She'd finally be everything that, before the pool, she'd always dreamed about and, after the pool, hadn't allowed herself to dream about. She wasn't sure how to put it into words. "After . . . well, after I came here, I thought a rejected familiar was all I'd ever be. I didn't think I'd get a second chance."

Those were miraculous words: *a second chance.*

"Familiars . . . They have the power to make lives better," Holly said. "Look at Calla — she and her wizard saved dozens of creatures from an avalanche. And have you heard the story of Quill and the baby sea turtles? Or Ash and his wizard — they subdued a basilisk before it could hurt anyone. If I had a second chance to become a familiar, I could make a real difference in animals' lives."

"What about the shelter and all the shelterlings?" Periwinkle asked. "After Charlie casts his spell, what will happen to this place?"

Holly stopped packing berries. "What do you mean?"

"If there are no more rejected familiars, then there's no need for the Shelter for Rejected Familiars," Periwinkle said. "Will everyone leave? Will there be no more shelterlings?"

Holly hadn't thought about that. She squirmed, not liking that idea. She pictured the strawberry patch, the orchard, the porch with its pillow-laden nest, the peonies in the yard, and the chairs in the living room. "Well, I don't know. I guess we'll have to see . . ."

"What do you think will happen?"

She imagined herself marching back to the Wizards Tower, demanding to retake the test, and being chosen by a wizard. Maybe multiple wizards would want her, and she'd get to choose. That would be amazing! After that, she'd accompany her wizard on adventures, going wherever they were needed the most. The other shelterlings would too!

At that thought, a question popped into her head: If she and Gus bonded with different wizards, would they still be able to be together? What if their wizards went on separate quests?

Holly didn't like where these thoughts were leading her. *It will all work out*, she told herself. She was sure of it. Anyway, that was such a faraway, *later* problem. First they had to find the crystal. She should be concentrating on helping with that challenge by finishing packing the snacks.

"How do you know it will make you happy?" Periwinkle asked. "I thought drinking from the Moon Mirror would fix my problems. But it didn't. I was still me."

"It'll make us all happy," Holly said.

"Are you sure?" Periwinkle scurried off the counter and then climbed back up with three paws. She held a piece of paper with her fourth. She dropped the paper next to the snack packs. "Look at this and tell me whether casting it is the right thing to do. If you say it is, I'll believe you."

Holly peered at the paper. "Periwinkle, where did you . . ." It was the spell, Charlie's spell for fixing the magic of the Moon Mirror. She touched the ragged edge of the paper. "You didn't —"

"I told you I steal stuff."

"But . . . from *Charlie?*"

"He yelled at you on the train," Periwinkle said. "You. The nicest animal I have ever met in my life. And he *yelled* at you. Why did he do that?"

"Because it was private, and I shouldn't have touched it!"

"Or because he has some secret he doesn't want you to know. Like maybe the spell won't really work. Or maybe he's not so sure what exactly it will do. Maybe it'll make the Moon Mirror worse instead of better. Or cause it to vanish altogether. Or change the water into, I don't know, all soap bubbles. Or mud. The other lemurs called me a pest for not just doing what I was told, but I don't think it's a bad thing to ask questions and think for yourself. I don't trust him. I trust you, though. If you say to cast the spell, then we'll cast the spell."

She said "we," Holly thought. And then her tail twitched as she considered what Periwinkle had said. The lemur's words were so close to what Holly herself had been worrying about. She tried to push her unease to the side.

Whether or not the spell was going to work was a separate issue from the fact that the lemur shouldn't have the piece of paper at all.

"It's his spell! You ripped it out of his notebook!" He'd made it very clear on the train that his notebook was personal and private. "Periwinkle, you shouldn't have done that."

Periwinkle shrugged. "If you're going to punish me for it, first you have to catch me!" She leaped off the counter, and Holly heard her running up the stairs.

Holly didn't chase her.

Touching the paper with a paw, she wondered if Periwinkle was right to ask her questions. Would she truly be happier if they fixed the water and fixed their magic? Would she be happier away from the shelter, away from Gus and all her other friends?

She thought again of Charlie's reaction when she had asked him to share the spell.

Maybe if I knew exactly how the spell worked, I'd feel better about all of this.

She could do what she should have done earlier, if she'd been brave enough in the face of his anger: ask him. And once he'd explained, she'd return the spell that Periwinkle had stolen. He'd be angry, but she'd explain that the little lemur had only wanted to help. Periwinkle was still learning the finer details of privacy and ownership and, well, not stealing stuff. She'd meant well. He'd understand, if she explained it.

Leaving the snacks and the spell, Holly hopped off the counter and hurried to the living room. The shelterlings were chattering — some excited, some worried. Everyone had an opinion and was expressing it loudly.

A few were marveling at the magic items. Charlie was encouraging them to hold the heart-shaped stone from the volcano and to smell the golden flower. He was proud of each ingredient they'd collected.

Nearby, Clover still had her head through the window. Tangerine was praising her for having practiced so much. It was nice to see the prophetic cow proud of herself.

Hesitating in the doorway, Holly wanted to join them and feel excited too. But instead she felt as if she'd gnawed on a moldy nut, as Periwinkle's words popped into her head: *Because he has some secret he doesn't want you to know* . . . There was only one way to get the bad taste out of her mouth. She had to spit it out. No more delaying. She had to talk to him.

"Charlie?" she called.

The noise of the others was too loud. No one heard her, except for Gus, who glided across the room and landed next to her. "Are you okay?" Gus asked. "You look upset."

"I . . ." Holly wasn't ready to put her concerns into words, and anyway, she didn't want to worry him unnecessarily. "I just have a question for Charlie." She raised her voice again. "Charlie, can I talk to you please? In the kitchen?"

The beaver waddled over. "Yes, my dear?"

She led him away from the hubbub. When the voices receded, she faced Charlie, took a deep breath, and asked, "Charlie . . . what is it you don't want me to know?"

"Whatever do you mean? There's nothing I don't want you to know. You're my friend. What kind of friend would I be if I kept secrets from you?"

That was the question, wasn't it? "The spell you plan on casting . . . are you sure it will work?"

"Of course, it will!"

"How? I saw the glyphs for the spell, and I saw you'd rewritten them. Can you explain to me what you changed and how it works?"

"You don't need to worry about the details," Charlie said.

"Answer me or . . . or . . . I won't let you bring these snacks." She winced at herself. She wasn't used to making threats. "You can have the snacks, but I want to know the truth. Do you really understand the spell? Are you completely certain it's correct?"

He hesitated ever so slightly. "Of course!"

"The truth, Charlie, please — what does the spell do, exactly? What aren't you telling us? Is it really going to fix the Moon Mirror, or are you just guessing? Why did you make changes to it? How do you know you're right and that this isn't a mistake?"

"The truth is as I said: I will fix everything for all of us," Charlie said.

"But how? The notes I saw —"

"You shouldn't have been looking in my personal notebook."

"I only read it because I wanted to help. And I can't unread it. So please, tell me what it means. Explain the spell to me." If he could just describe what each glyph did, she was sure she'd feel better about all of it.

"It uses the items we gathered to refuel the Moon Mirror."

"But how?"

He wiggled his paws. "Magic."

"Charlie!"

"We lay all the ingredients before the pool and say the words of the spell. That will activate the items. It's quite simple once you have the right ingredients and the right words."

"And the changes you made to the spell?"

"To make it stronger," Charlie said. "That's all. I want to make sure it doesn't fail."

"But what if —"

Charlie pleaded, "No *buts*. Holly, I don't understand why you're slowing us down. We have the answer! We can find the final ingredient! You can't flinch now."

"I'm not," Holly said. She just wanted to understand why he'd hidden the spell from her and why he still wouldn't explain exactly how it worked.

"This is our chance to make things better! Don't you want to make things better? Of course you do! I know you, Holly. You always try to do the right thing. Come, do the right thing with me."

She shook her head. Her oldest friend, her mentor, was pleading with her. This was *Charlie*. She didn't want to argue with him. She wanted to believe that he knew what he was doing and that he'd thought through all the consequences of his actions. He was wise. So maybe she was the one who was mistaken?

Crouching down, Charlie took her paws in his. His vastly larger ones fully enveloped hers. "I'll retrieve the crystal. I'll cast the spell. I'll take care of everything. You don't need to worry about it. Come to Cloud Mountain with me, watch me cast the spell, and you'll see!"

"I only want to make sure we're doing the right thing," Holly mumbled.

"Of course we are. Just think: in a few days' time, you won't be a 'rejected familiar' anymore!"

That was what she'd always wanted, to be a real familiar. How many times had she imagined herself traveling with her own wizard, helping those in need?

Charlie continued. "If your own future isn't enough to inspire you, then think of your friends. Think of their lives, their feelings. An accident condemned them to be useless mistakes. Trapped forever as neither ordinary nor a familiar. We can free them from their miserable state at last."

Maybe he's right, she thought. Besides, Charlie would never lead them astray. If he thought this was necessary, maybe it was. "I guess . . ."

He patted her on the head. "I'm glad we got that sorted out. Now, it's time for the final quest!" Leaving her alone in the kitchen, he returned to the living room. "Periwinkle? Where's my favorite lemur? Ah, my dear, ready for another adventure?"

Holly climbed back up to the counter and stared at the spell.

She should return it, she knew.

But he hadn't answered her questions.

CHAPTER FIFTEEN

Holly nibbled on her claws as she studied the spell. She didn't know why she hadn't returned it to Charlie, or why she still didn't. She kept staring at the glyphs as if that would suddenly make her able to read them.

The only shelterling who could read glyphs this complicated was Charlie, and he clearly wasn't going to help her. Plus, she'd have to tell him why she'd kept the spell instead of returning it immediately, and she didn't have a good explanation for that.

She conjured a croissant and began chewing on it instead of her claws. Of course, Charlie wasn't the only one who could read spells. A familiar who'd studied spells could do it. As it happened, she knew a familiar: Saffron.

He'd said that if she ever needed anything, she shouldn't hesitate to ask. She was sure he'd help. She was also sure she knew where to find him. Unless he was off on another quest, he'd be at the Wizards Tower.

I could pop over there, ask Saffron to read the glyphs to me and explain Charlie's notes — or point me in the direction of someone who can read them, if he can't — and then pop back, before Charlie even knows the spell is missing, Holly thought. She could ask Periwinkle to slide it back into his satchel when he wasn't looking.

Or she could simply tell the truth, that she was sorry for keeping the spell but she'd wanted to be certain she was making the right choice, and would he please forgive her.

What harm would there be in that?

She knew how to get to the Wizards Tower. The arrival circle went both ways. Going would, however, mean returning to the place she'd never wanted to see again. But it was the most sensible option, given the fact that she wasn't going to stop worrying about this. Let Saffron tell her that everything was fine and that the spell would work exactly as Charlie said, and then Holly could proceed with a clear mind and heart.

After rolling up the spell, she tucked it under her chin and headed outside. She heard the others continuing to talk, plan, and argue in the living room, but she didn't pause.

Outside, the sun was obscured by clouds, making the peonies look dull. She trotted to the circle of rocks. She didn't have to know how to read these glyphs to work them. All she had to do was touch each one to activate it.

Holly ran from stone to stone, tapping each glyph with a paw.

The stones began to glow white, and then purple sparkles teased the corners of her eyes. The sparkles thickened, and soon her fur was coated in them. Holding up one paw, she saw that it looked pale. Soon she could see through it to the stones on the opposite side.

She was going.

She took a deep breath. Through the haze of purple, she saw Gus glide out of the upstairs window. Faintly, she heard him call to her, and she waved so he wouldn't worry.

Then everything was just purple.

✦

When the sparkles faded, Holly was standing in a circle of stones identical to the one at the shelter, except that instead of facing a tidy lawn with peony bushes and a trellis, she saw a white stone tower so high that she had to squint to see the top.

She waited for the moment that the memories would slam into her.

But, oddly, they didn't. Of course she remembered coming here after drinking from the magic pool — she'd entered on foot that time, through the east gate, and had presented herself to a badger who was in charge of all visitors to the Wizards Tower. His primary role was to vet requests for wizardly assistance and pass those appeals onto the wizards and their familiars, but he also handled any animal who wanted to become a familiar. He'd recorded her name on a list, and she'd waited in a garden near the door to the tower . . .

Carrying the spell, Holly headed for the entrance. She remembered the garden as being extravagant: neat and organized in a way that her home forest never was, with all the yellow flowers corralled together, all the white roses contained to neatly manicured bushes, and all the trees pruned into symmetrical shapes.

This time, though, as she gazed around the garden, she wasn't as impressed. It was still lovely, but she thought the shelter gardens were equally fine. For one thing, the shelterlings grew fruits and vegetables. The Wizards Tower had no strawberry patch. All the plants were ornamental. Also, she thought the trees looked a bit too trimmed, as if they were unhappy they weren't able to sprawl the way they wanted.

The same badger she remembered scurried over toward her. This was going to be humiliating. He was going to remind her how she'd been judged useless and didn't belong here with others who —

"Do you require the services of a wizard and familiar?" he asked.

"Not exactly, but I —"

"Then are you here to apply to become a familiar? If you are, I must record your name." He produced a notebook and held a pen ready in his hand. He waited for her to respond.

"No, I'm not . . ." *He doesn't remember me*, she realized. He didn't care that she'd failed before. The most painful, disappointing day of her life, and he had no idea he'd witnessed it. He was the one who'd explained that she was a shelterling now. And he was the one who'd activated the glyphs on the circle to send her to the shelter. Yet he wasn't looking at her with any sign of recognition at all. "I'm looking for a familiar named Saffron," she said. "Not for a quest, though. I only want to speak with him. Is he here?"

"Saffron . . . Saffron . . ." The badger checked his notes.

She wasn't sure if it made it better or worse that he seemed to have no idea who Saffron was either. She waited while he found the name.

"Ah, yes, third floor, room thirty-six." Spotting another visitor, a human in a carriage, the badger trotted out of the garden without another word. She stared after him.

Maybe that terrible day hadn't been as important as she'd believed.

Or maybe the badger just has a terrible memory, she thought.

Holly followed his directions into the tower and jumped up step after step until she reached the third floor. The doors were all shut, and she wasn't certain which was thirty-six. She didn't see any numbers or markings anywhere.

But she did hear voices from behind one:

"Get this. She actually said" — the voice adopted a higher, more nasal pitch — "'You can play fetch while I finish up.' Fetch! As if I did all this to play."

Another voice said, "Rude. Mine never lets me choose quests either. I told him, 'Don't say we'll do the desert. You hate the heat. I shed.' But what did he do? Said yes. And then whined the entire time about how much he hates the heat and how much my fur makes him sneeze. As if it's my fault I'm a mammal."

"He could have picked a lizard or a snake and let you bond with a wizard who didn't sneeze." That voice sounded familiar.

Scratching at the door, she called, "Saffron? Saffron, are you here? Excuse me?"

Through the door, she heard, "Who's asking?"

The first voice called, "Who is it, Saffron?"

Pushing open a cat-size flap in the base of the door, the cat Saffron peered out at her.

"Oh! Hi," Holly said. "I'm not sure if you remember me —"

"Holly? Of course I remember you. You saved my life. That's not the kind of thing you forget. Are you all right? What brings you here?" Before Holly could answer, the cat shooed her inside. "Come in. Make yourself comfortable."

"Thanks," Holly said. "Everything's fine, and it's probably silly that I came —"

"Nonsense," Saffron said.

A black cat lounging on the windowsill said, "What's silly is that Saffron got caught in a cobweb like a bug."

On the floor, by a stack of books, a shaggy dog laughed so hard his ears shook.

"You're not going to let me forget that, are you?" Saffron said. "It could have happened to anyone. That's what I keep trying to tell my wizard. She's mortified that she was the victim of a sleep spell."

"Facing a dragon isn't anything to be embarrassed about," Holly said.

Saffron snorted. "Yeah, well, she's been unbearable ever since, refusing to take on any more quests and sulking all day — but I'm being impolite. Everyone, this is my friend Holly."

The black cat slunk off the windowsill and circled around her. "Holly . . . So you're the rejected familiar that Saffron told us about?"

He'd talked about her? She wondered what he'd said. "Yes?"

"Impressive work," the shaggy dog said. "I'm Moss."

"Moonlight," the cat introduced herself.

"Nice to meet you," Holly said. She'd never been in a room with three familiars before. She'd also never been in a room that belonged to a wizard and a familiar. She looked around. It was stuffed with books and scrolls. They were crammed into shelves, teetering in piles, and shoved beneath furniture. One table was made entirely of books, and another was covered in them. A chair — if it was a chair — was buried beneath papers.

Pillows were also scattered throughout the room. Several were piled on a couch that Holly thought either served as the human wizard's bed or a really large bird's nest, and others were strewn between towers of books and were covered in cat hair.

"We always thought rejected familiars couldn't handle adventures," Moonlight said. "That's why they weren't chosen. Not powerful enough. Not brave enough."

Moss growled. "You're insulting the squirrel."

"I was leading to a compliment!" Moonlight said. "I was going to say, before I was interrupted, that I am happy to have been proved wrong. Saffron said that you and your companion were, of your own volition, seeking out a magic flower. You chose your own quest."

"We . . . did." Holly hadn't thought of it in those terms, but the cat was right.

"And I bet no one told *you* to play fetch," Moss said.

"All right," Saffron said. "You've both met her now. Curiosity satisfied. Now let me talk to her. She came here for a reason, and it wasn't to listen to us gripe."

Both Moss and Moonlight exited with a polite "nice to meet you." She watched them go. She hadn't thought familiars would be so . . . friendly. She wanted to ask them questions — what it was like to be bonded with a wizard, what kind of quests they'd gone on, and whether they were happy. But that wasn't why she was here.

"So, what's wrong?" Saffron asked her.

"Nothing," Holly said quickly. "Probably nothing. That is, I was hoping you could read a variant on a spell for me and tell me what it all means." She held out the rolled-up piece of paper. "Can you read the glyphs?"

The cat took it carefully with his claws, laid it on the floor, and flattened it with his paws. He leaned over it so closely his whiskers brushed the page.

While he studied the glyphs, Holly waited. Tumbleweeds of cat hair drifted by as a breeze blew in from the open window. Holly resisted the urge to begin sweeping with her tail. She'd expected a wizard and familiar's home to be . . . well, at least neater.

She looked back at the cat, who was pressed up against the spell even closer now and muttering, "Hmm, hmm, clever, hmm."

At last, he looked up. "Where did you get this?"

"My friend Charlie."

"Ah, and you want to give him your magic?"

"What? No!" She scurried next to him and peered down at the spell. "It's not supposed to do that at all. You must have misread it."

Saffron sniffed. "Do you know how many hours I've spent studying spell books?"

"Sorry, but it's supposed to be a spell to fix the Moon Mirror."

She pointed with her paw at the glyphs. "It's supposed to recast the spell of our ancestors, the one that infused the water with magic in the first place. What I want to know is will it work, what will it do, and will it change our lives?"

He laid his paw lightly on the glyphs. "Well, it will certainly change your life. These glyphs here are the original spell. See?" He read them for her. "If you repeat the conditions of the original spell — go to the top of Cloud Mountain with a group of animals, lay all seven ingredients at the edge of the pool, and say these words together — you'll recast the original spell, though I don't know why you'd want to. Regardless, if you look at the altered spell . . . See here. And here." He pointed to the glyphs in Charlie's handwriting, on the back of the original spell. "These alter the intent of the spell. And these determine the target. With these changes, the altered spell uses the Moon Mirror to funnel magic from any animal who has touched the ingredients into one central spell caster."

Holly felt ill. Worse than if she'd eaten a moldy nut. "He said his changes would just strengthen the original spell."

"He lied to you," Saffron said.

She squeezed her eyes shut and said in a small voice, "No. Not Charlie."

"The alterations on this spell . . . they're too precise to be an accident. These are deliberate changes. A real nasty bit of work. You say this is a friend of yours? What wizard is he bonded with? Very surprised any wizard would allow this. It's not what I'd call an ethical spell."

"He's a rejected familiar," Holly said. "Like me. All he can do is conjure flowers."

Saffron snorted. "I'd say he plans to do a good bit more after he casts this spell. It will give him the combined power of all involved. But you don't need to worry."

"I don't?" It sounded as if she very much needed to worry. All of them did.

"See this glyph?" He pointed with a claw to a glyph that looked like a seven-legged spider. "This enables the spell to affect creatures who have handled the ingredients. So if you haven't touched any of the magic items, you'll be safe."

Holly felt worse by the minute. Was that why Charlie had insisted he needed their help in finding the ingredients? So they would be sure to handle them? At this point, she was certain that nearly every shelterling had touched them — to admire them, if nothing else. She pictured Charlie in the living room, encouraging all the shelterlings to hold the meteorite, to touch the rock from the volcano, to smell the magic flower. She'd thought he'd been proud of their success, but it was all a part of his plan.

"And even if you have," Saffron said quickly, as if he could tell by her expression that she had, "you still don't need to worry. The spell requires all seven ingredients. They act as amplifiers, you see." He pointed to another glyph. "Without them, your spell won't be strong enough for your 'friend' to do any damage. And all seven of these are rare. Very tricky to get."

"He has all but one ingredient." With Periwinkle's help, he'd soon have the last one, if Holly didn't make it back to the shelter in time to stop him. Scooping up the spell, she ran out of Saffron's room. "Thank you so much! Come to the shelter sometime, after this is over, and you can have some of our strawberries! They're the best!"

"Um, okay, thanks," Saffron said. "You know cats don't eat strawberries, right?"

"Then I'll conjure you a croissant!"

His voice followed her. "Cats also don't eat croissants . . ."

She hurried down the stairs, leaping as she went and holding the spell tight against her. She didn't know what she was going to say to Charlie, or how to explain to everyone that he planned to betray them, but she knew she had to get back as quickly as possible.

She sped past the badger toward the arrival circle. Quickly, she tapped each of the stones with her paws and tail. The purple sparkles began to appear.

Faster! she thought at the sparkles. *Go faster!*

Chapter Sixteen

When the purple sparkles cleared, Holly darted out of the arrival circle toward the shelter. "Charlie! Charlie, come out! I have to talk to you!" She ran past a statue of an owl and then skidded to a stop. "Gus, where's Charlie?"

The gray seeped from the owl's face, and he transformed back into flesh and feathers. "Holly, you're back! I saw you in the arrival circle. Did you go to the Wizards Tower? Why?"

"I need to talk to Charlie," Holly said. "And Periwinkle. Right now!"

"What's wrong?"

Words failed her, and she made a chittering noise that was close to a sob. "He — he —" She needed to understand why Charlie would betray them like this. Maybe he could explain. Maybe there was a reason. Or maybe he could tell her it was all a misunderstanding, and he never intended to cast anything but the original spell. He could have made a mistake with his additional glyphs. He might not have known what they'd do. But even as she thought it, she didn't believe it. *He didn't make a mistake,* she thought. That was just wishful thinking. "I have to ask him why!"

She darted into the house, through the kitchen, the living room, up through the ribbons in Periwinkle's room — and then out again. The other shelterlings called to her, but she didn't stop. She raced outside again to Gus and demanded, "Where's Charlie?"

"Whoa, slow down," Gus said. "He and Periwinkle left shortly after you did. Periwinkle wanted to wait for you, but then the train whistle blew —"

Letting out a high-pitched squeak, Holly bolted out through the trellis and pelted across the field. How long ago had they left? Had the train come yet? She'd meant to be quick. She shouldn't have lingered in the tower garden, slowed by her memories.

Halfway across the meadow, she realized she couldn't see or hear the train. It had already come and gone. "I'm too late!" she wailed. She ran in a tight circle. Now what would she do? They were already gone! *This is terrible*, she thought. *Awful. Horrible. A disaster!*

Gus glided after her, then flew past to land a few feet away. "Holly, what's going on? Please, take a breath, calm down, and talk to me."

She pivoted and ran back toward the shelter. "Charlie's betrayed us!"

"What?"

"We have to stop him!"

By the time she reached the yard, the other shelterlings were emerging: trotting, flying, and slithering out to see what was going on.

Holly looked at all her friends and at their home. The peonies were still plump and pink, the yard was perfectly green, and she could see a corner of the strawberry patch around the corner of the house. It all looked beautiful. But everything felt wrong, wrong, wrong.

"Holly, please," Gus said, "tell us what happened?"

Quickly Holly explained where she'd gone and what Saffron had said. She showed them the spell with Charlie's glyphs and summarized what she'd learned: "Unless Saffron was wrong . . . unless there's some other explanation . . . Charlie wants to take our magic and give it to himself."

Around her, the others gasped, and she knew she didn't think Saffron was mistaken or that there was another explanation. Charlie had written his altered spell with too much care and precision. He'd been too insistent that he needed all their help, even though, as Periwinkle had once pointed out, he could have retrieved some of the items himself. He'd been too protective of his notebook. All of it added up to the fact that their old friend was betraying them.

"My prophecies!" Clover cried.

"And my *hat*!" Bluebell moaned.

Yes, their magic wasn't perfect, but Bluebell loved being able to transform his beloved hat, and Zephyr loved racing as fast as he could. And Holly . . . She conjured a croissant and looked it over. Then she took a deep breath.

"We can't let him do it," Holly said. And those words felt right.

She'd never tried to stop anyone from doing anything before. She'd always been the helper, the negotiator, the one who soothed feelings and wanted to make everyone feel welcome. She was a *nice* squirrel.

But, for the first time in her life, she didn't feel like being nice.

He shouldn't be trying to steal our magic, Holly thought. *He's the one who isn't nice.*

"We can't let him cast the spell," Holly said even more firmly. She explained what Saffron had said: that the ingredients both amplified the spell and tied the shelterlings to it. "We have to destroy the other six ingredients. If we can get rid of them, then it won't matter that he and Periwinkle are already on their way to find the crystal. He needs them all."

"But Holly," Pepper piped up, "we can't do that."

"What do you mean?" Holly asked.

"He took all the other ingredients with him," Pepper said, flapping her wings in so much distress that pink feathers flew into the air. "He put them in his bag, along with the snacks."

Holly felt her stomach twist into a knot. Charlie hadn't wanted to risk that anyone would interfere with his grand plan. *We trusted him,* she thought, *but he never trusted us.*

"Zephyr, how many of us can you carry on your shell and still run fast?" Holly asked.

The turtle zipped forward, crashed into a bush, and then backed up. "I'm fast *and* strong, so I can carry as many as can fit . . . which admittedly isn't many, now that I think about it. Leaf and one other. So, two. Why? What do you have in mind?"

"We follow them," Holly said. "Catch up to them before it's too late."

Gus cheered. "Yes!"

"And when we catch them, we engage in battle most fierce?" Bluebell asked, boxing the air with his paws. As he hopped from side to side, he transformed his hat into a pointy helmet with a feather at its peak.

She didn't want to fight anyone. "First we talk to him."

"And then, O Most Wise Leader, we fight?" Bluebell asked. "Charlie will not surrender his prize merely because we ask."

"Periwinkle would help us, if she knew the truth," Holly said. After all, the lemur had stolen the spell in the first place — she must have suspected that all was not right. Or maybe she just didn't trust anyone. "She's only helping Charlie because she thinks it's what we want her to do. If we can get to her before they reach the cave and tell her what he plans, she won't find the crystal for him, and he won't be able to cast the spell."

"Periwinkle might even be able to get the other ingredients," Gus said. "We distract Charlie, you tell her the truth, and she hands them all over to you. Boom! It's over!"

"And then, once we have the ingredients, we can use them to cast the real spell," Tangerine said. "We can fix the Moon Mirror, the way he promised to."

He's right, Holly thought. If they could get the ingredients, then they could fix the pool. After all, she had the spell. *Maybe everything can still be okay, if we're quick enough.* She handed the paper with the spell to Tangerine. "Can you keep this safe?"

The porcupine stuck it onto his quills, taking care to only pierce the edges. Concentrating, he changed color, camouflaging the spell to match his quills. Holly asked, "Are there any volunteers to help Tangerine bring the spell to Cloud Mountain?"

Clover stepped forward. "He can ride on me."

"I'll fly with them as well," Pepper said.

"If you get there before us, guard the trail up to the Moon Mirror," Holly said. "If we fail at the Maw, it'll be up to you to stop Charlie from reaching the top of Cloud Mountain."

Pepper nodded her long pink neck. "We won't let you down."

"And I won't let all of you down," Holly told her friends.

"I can't fly as fast as Zephyr can run, but I'll follow you to the Maw," Gus said to Holly. "You might need backup."

Bluebell declared, "I relinquish my bard duties and instead volunteer for warrior service! I too will be a shield on your arm, a helmet for your head, and socks for your paws! I will follow as well."

I'm lucky to have all of them, Holly thought. "All right. Let's do this." To the other shelterlings, she said, "Wish us luck."

Clustering together, her friends waved and cheered. "Good luck!"

"Run fast," Holly told Zephyr.

"I can do that!" the turtle said.

✦

They sped across the field, over the train tracks, through a meadow, and along the river. Far in the distance, Holly could hear the train. It cut across the countryside, miles ahead of them.

"Can you go any faster?" Holly asked.

Clinging to the shell beside her, Leaf said, "I don't think that's a good —" He shrieked as Zephyr increased speed. "Ahh! My eyeballs are going to pop out!"

"Then close your eyes!" Zephyr said. "This is awesome!"

Holly held so tight to the edge of the shell that her paws ached, but she didn't dare loosen her grip. She kept an eye out for trees and rocks. Luckily, the way seemed to be clear —

"Watch out!" she shouted.

Zephyr hit a rock and sailed into the air.

He crashed down on the other side. Holly's teeth slammed together, and her chin hit his shell from the impact. But Zephyr didn't slow.

It was almost like flying with Gus, except bouncier and with a far greater danger of crashing. As they hurtled after the train, she began to think that riding on the turtle was *not* the best idea she'd ever had. There was no way to steer him. But if they slowed, they'd lose the train. And if they didn't . . . a tree or rock would definitely slow them down.

Go fast and crash, or go slow and fall behind — she didn't love the choices.

Zephyr hit another rock. "Sorry!"

He then skirted a tree, but only barely.

The train sped on ahead of them.

If only she had realized the truth about the spell sooner! But she'd wanted so badly to believe that her old friend had their best interests at heart. She'd certainly never imagined he'd do anything like this.

Leaf, his voice vibrating as he bounced on Zephyr's shell, said, "We can't catch them. They're on a train! We can't outrun a train!"

He's right, she admitted.

"They won't always be on a train," Zephyr called back.

Also right, she thought. The train only went to cities and towns, but no people lived on the Seven Sisters Mountains. At some point, Charlie and Periwinkle would disembark and continue by paw, and *that* was when they'd catch up and, hopefully, stop them, *if* they could keep from crashing before —

"Ahh, hold on!" Zephyr slammed into a hay bale, and they burst out the other side, tumbled across the pasture, and landed in a heap of cow manure. "Yuck."

Holly sat up. Manure was stuck to her fur and all along her tail. She tried to shake it off, and it spattered on the turtle and gecko. "Sorry!"

Grumbling, Leaf waddled to a puddle and plopped himself into it. "This is never going to work," he said. "Charlie was right about one thing — we're failures. Just like the wizards said."

Holly joined him in the puddle. She scrubbed at her fur, especially her tail, until she was at last, thankfully, clean. "We can't give up," she said to Leaf. "Everyone's counting on us." To Zephyr she said, "You're doing fine. You just need to work on your reaction speed."

Leaf snorted.

Zephyr jumped into the puddle, spraying water everywhere, and submerged himself. "I don't think we can catch them before they reach the mountain," he admitted when he came up for air.

"Then we'll be there when they come out," Holly said. She climbed back onto his shell. She shot a look at Leaf, who sighed and climbed on too. "You're only a failure if you quit," Holly said, thinking of Cerulean. "Until then, you're just someone who hasn't succeeded yet."

✦

Choices, Holly thought as they at last reached the mountains. It's always about choices: what kind of creature you choose to be. She'd chosen not to be an ordinary squirrel: to leave her forest and climb Cloud Mountain. She'd chosen to help the other shelterlings adjust to their new life and, when they wanted to, improve their powers. She'd always tried to choose to be kind. And Charlie had made a very different choice.

She couldn't let him succeed.

Crisp against the pale blue sky, mountains were displayed before them in all their glory. The Maw was the center mountain, its peak split into two rocky points that looked like jaws. It was edged with ice and snow, and its slope was blanketed in a thick forest of pine trees.

At the foot of the mountains was a clump of houses nestled between trees. Stopping on the crest of a hill, Holly and her friends looked down. The train tracks ran right into the heart of the town and ended at a platform beside a station. The train sat there, with smoke billowing out of its smokestack and then dispersing into the clouds above.

"Do you see them?" Zephyr asked.

Holly sat up higher on his shell for a better view. "Not yet."

With a whistle, the train pulled away from the station. Charlie and Periwinkle would have disembarked. Several humans milled on the train platform, but there — Yes! A beaver was waddling off the platform, following by a lemur who kept darting left and right, under benches and behind trash cans. A scarf flowed behind her, blowing gently in the mountain breeze.

"They're here," Holly said.

She was relieved. There was always the chance Charlie and Periwinkle could have taken a different route, found the crystal already, and be on their way to Cloud Mountain.

"Follow them," Holly ordered.

Leaf squeaked. "Wait, don't! There's too much to crash into in the town. They'll hear you coming way before we can reach them, and they'll escape while we're untangling ourselves from whatever tree or trash can."

"But if I don't run —" Zephyr objected.

"We have to sneak," Leaf insisted.

"He's right," Holly said. If Charlie heard them coming, he could disappear into the forest beyond the town and lose them between the trees. They could end up flailing around on the side of the mountain while Charlie found the crystal without them. "Maybe we'll have a chance to catch up when we're closer to the cave."

Without racing, the turtle, squirrel, and gecko hurried around the town and into the pine forest. They located the spot where the beaver and lemur had entered the woods and plunged into the forest after them.

Holly's nose twitched as she inhaled the scent of pine trees and alpine flowers. She felt the wind ruffle her fur. Every time they doubted their direction, she'd scamper up the nearest tree.

At last, from the top of her fifth tree, Holly glimpsed a cave. She saw the silhouettes of Charlie and Periwinkle — too far away to see clearly, but unmistakable in their shapes — disappear into the darkness.

Pressing on, Holly, Zephyr, and Leaf reached the mouth of the cave.

"Now what?" Leaf asked.

"We wait," Holly said.

Chapter Seventeen

Holly couldn't stop her thoughts from running in circles: What if they couldn't get the ingredients from Charlie, what if he succeeded in stealing their magic, what did he plan to do with all their magic, and what would happen to them?

Zephyr zipped back and forth in front of the cave mouth, ricocheting off rocks. "When are they going to come out? We've been waiting for *hours* and *hours*."

"Minutes," Leaf corrected.

"It feels like hours."

Leaf peered into the shadows of the cave. His tongue flicked in and out, tasting the air. "What if they can't find it?"

"Then I guess we have nothing to worry about," Holly said.

"What if they do find it and leave through another exit?" Leaf asked.

"Then we *do* have something to worry about," Holly said. Her tail twitched. "I don't know! I'm as new to this as you are."

Zephyr sped past the entrance again. "How about I zip in there, grab the ingredients from them, and zip out before they have the chance to stop me?"

"That's a terrible idea," Leaf said. "You can't steer yourself when you run in daylight with your eyes wide open. What if you run into a crevasse? Or into a cave wall? Or several cave walls? What if you cause a cave-in? What if you get lost?"

"All excellent questions. But, counterpoint: it would be fun."

Again, Leaf was right about Zephyr's limitations. There was too much potential for disaster if the turtle went careening into the cave too fast to follow Clover's directions. "We wait," Holly said firmly.

Zephyr splayed out his legs and plopped onto his belly with a sigh. Absently, he spun himself in a circle. A few minutes later, he said, "They could be lost."

"They could be," Holly admitted.

"I hate waiting," Zephyr said. "I've already wasted too much time waiting. Waiting to hatch. Waiting to grow. Waiting for spring. My mother used to say, 'Slow and steady is best. It's the turtle way.' But I want to do things *my* way. I never want to wait for things to happen to me. I want to be the one to make things happen!"

Holly understood that. Especially waiting for spring, waiting for life to begin again, waiting for something to happen that would make her feel as if she was living the life she was meant to live . . . "I'll go in and get them," she said.

"Hey, didn't you hear my speech? I want to do it!"

"You need to stay out here," Holly said. "If Charlie emerges, you're the only one fast enough to grab the ingredients from him."

"But what if you get lost?" Leaf asked.

She had an idea for that. Concentrating, she generated a croissant. It popped into existence in her open paws. "I'll leave myself a trail. Even if I can't see it, I'll be able to smell it."

Holly plucked a paw-size crumb off the croissant, dropped it at the cave entrance, and then trotted inside. She kept dropping crumbs as she crept farther into the cave.

Shadows enveloped her, but a thin sliver of light from the entrance illuminated the rock walls. As she ventured deeper, she widened her eyes, feeling a bit like a lemur.

Soon she reached a branch in the cave. Right or left?

Peering down each tunnel, she couldn't see more than a few feet in either direction. The thin bit of sunlight couldn't pierce the shadows. She thought of Clover's directions.

"The path you seek kind of reeks," she murmured.

She sniffed the air.

In the right tunnel, she smelled a musty kind of mildew, like in the basement of the shelter. She tried the left tunnel. It smelled . . . a little nicer, she thought. Fresher.

Continuing on, she dropped more bits of croissant. She sniffed as she crept closer, letting the hint of fresh air guide her. Soon the darkness deepened until everything looked like shadows.

She felt the tunnel begin to climb up, and she stopped. The next direction was to go up, up, up, which meant she had to go down, down, down. Backtracking, she felt with her paws until she found a bit of the cave that dipped down.

The rock beneath her paws felt damp and cool. The air tasted odd too — coppery, like a coin. She scraped her tongue against her teeth, as if that would get rid of the taste of the air.

Just when she thought she couldn't stand the dark any longer, she saw a hint of light, and she remembered the third bit of direction: to head to the dark, which meant she should do the opposite. Grateful, she hurried toward the light and saw that it came from above: a slit in the rock that opened to the sky.

That was as far as Clover's directions had gone, so Charlie and Periwinkle should be nearby. Stopping, she flicked her ears forward and listened. The only sound was a steady *drip-drip-drip* from water. She didn't hear any hint of the lemur and the beaver. Using the bit of light from above, she examined the ground, looking for paw prints, but she couldn't see any sign that they'd come this way.

She began to wonder if she'd made a mistake. She didn't know how many tunnels there were inside the Maw, or which one Periwinkle and Charlie had chosen to follow. What if she'd gone the wrong way? Or what if they had? What if she'd already passed them? What if they'd exited the cave, and she'd missed her chance to save the day? "Periwinkle?" she whispered.

Her voice echoed and then disappeared as if swallowed by the mountain.

She thought about the amount of rock that was above, below, and on all sides of her. So much rock. She tried instead to think about flying and acorns and parsnip soup and sunlight and other things that made her happy.

She wished she hadn't come in here alone. She'd felt so certain she was doing the right thing when she'd plunged into the shadows with her conjured croissant, but maybe she shouldn't have left Leaf and Zephyr outside. Maybe she should have waited for Gus and Bluebell to arrive.

Maybe I should turn around, she thought.

She'd left a trail. She could follow it.

Pivoting, she sniffed the air. But the buttery scent was all over her front paws. It drowned out any smell from the crumbs.

I know I dropped them, she thought.

Maybe she should have dropped more. She'd gotten excited when she'd seen the light. She should have thought about the fact that she'd have to find her trail again. Zigzagging, she searched for the crumbs. What if she never found them? What if she couldn't find her way back? What if —

"Hi, Holly!" a little voice chirped behind her.

"Periwinkle?" Holly jumped and spun around, trying to pinpoint the source of the voice. She peered into the shadows. She couldn't help a little hitch in her voice. "I . . . I got a little lost."

"Yeah, I can tell," Periwinkle said cheerfully. She emerged into the strip of light. "You're glowing as brightly as the moon. In fact, we all are."

"We?" Holly asked.

The beaver's voice rumbled as he lumbered out of the darkness to join Periwinkle. "Unfortunately, we haven't yet found the way out."

In a smaller voice, Periwinkle said, "I'm trying."

"I know you are, my dear." His voice was still jovial, but somehow that made it worse. There wasn't enough light for Holly to see his face. He was a great hulking shadow beside the lemur. "But perhaps you could try a little harder?"

"Yes, Charlie."

"I left crumbs . . . but then I lost them," Holly said. "If you search for them . . ."

On all fours, Periwinkle passed her, examining every inch of the tunnel. Soon it was just Holly and Charlie in the patch of light. She noticed that Charlie wore his satchel. It was a bulging shadow on his side. At least six ingredients were in there, she guessed. Probably all seven. "Did you find the crystal?" she asked.

Down the tunnel, Periwinkle's voice bounced through the cave. "I did!" she said happily. "Charlie can show you when we're out of these caves. It was exactly where Clover had said it would be, or where she said it wouldn't be. There are more openings as you continue on — we just followed the light, and there it was!"

"So we have all the ingredients," Holly said, and tried to sound cheerful about it. She wondered if Charlie had noticed the missing spell yet — if so, did he suspect who had it?

"Holly," Charlie said, "why are you here? I specifically told everyone that I only needed Periwinkle with me on this adventure. All of you had already done enough."

You mean we've already touched the other ingredients, she thought. *We're already tied to the spell*. She took a deep breath. This was it. She'd wanted a chance to talk to him, to give Charlie an opportunity to explain that Saffron was wrong and he wasn't planning to betray them, and now he'd given her an opening. She had to seize it. "I needed to ask you a question."

"So badly that you chased after me all the way here and got yourself lost inside a cave?" Charlie sounded amused, but in the partial darkness, the beaver looked even larger than he was. He was an ominous shadow.

"Why did you lie to us?" she asked.

"Lie? I would never!"

"Then why did you alter the spell to steal our magic and take it for yourself?"

Farther along the tunnel, she heard the scuffle of pebbles. Periwinkle called, "What was that?"

"How did you —" Charlie cut himself off. "Everything's fine," he told Periwinkle. "Keep looking for a way out."

Holly heard Periwinkle's paw steps fade as she scampered farther away from them.

In a lower voice, he said to Holly, "You make it sound like I'm doing something bad. But I'm righting a wrong. I'm fixing an injustice."

For an instant, she couldn't breathe. In her heart of hearts, she hadn't expected him to just admit it. She'd expected an explanation, or at least an excuse. *Oh, Charlie, I trusted you!*

"You have no use for your magic," Charlie said. "It's done nothing but make you miserable, stuck as you are between ordinary animals and true familiars. But if you gave it to me . . . Think of it, Holly: with the combined magic of the shelterlings —

magic that's currently serving no purpose — I will be the first animal powerful enough to achieve miracles without a wizard! After I cast my spell, it won't matter what the wizards think or say. I will be Charlie, the familiar who needs no wizard! I will be legendary!"

Even though she'd known he was guilty, it still hurt to hear this. He'd been one of her oldest, dearest friends at the shelter, and she'd looked up to him. After he'd left, she'd tried to be like him, the heart of the shelter —

"You said you'd fix the Moon Mirror and we could become familiars! Instead, you're betraying us," she said.

"Well, Holly, that's a bit melodramatic, don't you think? I didn't lie to you. I simply didn't tell you all the details. I promised you wouldn't be rejected familiars anymore. And you won't. You can go back to the lives you were supposed to lead. Come now. You have to admit that none of you are happy as you are."

"But —"

"I know you want to be freed of being rejected familiars," Charlie said. "Why else would it have been so easy for me to trick all of you? You *wanted* to be tricked. You wanted to be saved from the unhappiness you've been living in." His voice softened. He was close to her, so close she could feel the warmth of his breath even though he didn't touch her. "This isn't just about me. It's about making all the shelterlings happy."

"How do you know whether we're happy or not?" Holly asked. "You left the shelter. You don't know us or what our lives are like!"

"How can you be anything but miserable? You're failures. Neither ordinary nor a familiar. You're *nothing*. And arguing serves no purpose. You're already linked to the spell. All that remains is for me to cast it."

"You can't!" Holly said triumphantly. "You don't have the spell! And you'll never get it back." She was glad she'd given it to Tangerine, who would keep it safely camouflaged on his quills. They'd never let Charlie find it.

The beaver laughed.

She shivered, unsure why that was so funny.

"Oh, my sweet squirrel," Charlie said, "do you really think I need that scrap of paper? I have the spell memorized, of course. I have waited and worked patiently and tirelessly for this moment, and now, at last, it's my time. You can't stop this. It's going to happen. You may as well accept it."

Ahead of them, Periwinkle let out a yelp, and Holly heard the scrambling of paws on rocks. "I found them!" the lemur cried. "Your crumbs!" There were more sounds of paws on pebbles, echoing through the tunnel. "I found the way out! Follow my voice. This way . . . this way . . ."

Holly followed the sound of Periwinkle's voice. So did Charlie. They moved quickly through the tunnels, with the lemur urging them onward. Holly's searching paw touched one of her croissant crumbs and then another.

Ahead she saw a sliver of light. The sun!

"Zephyr, get Charlie's bag!" Holly cried.

Just as they emerged into the blindingly bright sunlight, Zephyr darted forward, grabbed Charlie's satchel in his mouth, and kept running until he sailed off the side of the mountain.

Clinging to Zephyr's shell, Leaf puffed up. Their fall slowed until they hovered only a few feet away from the side of the mountain.

"I got it," Zephyr said, the words muffled by the bag.

"Great! And I got you," Leaf said.

Sinking lower and lower, they floated closer to the ground. Leaf couldn't hold him for long — not without Gus to help. Any second now, Zephyr and Leaf would sink to the turf.

Charlie ran toward them, ready to catch them when they dipped low enough.

Holly scurried up into a pine tree and yelled, "Be careful!"

"If you can steer us away from Charlie before we land, I can run us away," Zephyr said, muffled around the satchel. There wasn't any wind — Leaf should be able to control their course.

"What about Holly and Periwinkle?" Leaf asked.

"We'll be fine," Holly said. "Just get the ingredients to safety!"

Periwinkle climbed up next to Holly. "What are you doing? Holly, what's going on? What were you and Charlie talking about? What did he do?"

Puffing air out and paddling with his toes, Leaf began to drift back toward the cave entrance — closer to Charlie. Zephyr swam through the air with his stubby legs, but they were drifting lower and lower. "Gah!"

No, no, no, Holly thought. They had to get far away.

The beaver jumped, swiping his paw toward the bag and missing. "Give that back!"

"We have to go higher!" Zephyr cried. "We're too heavy."

"Give me the bag," Leaf said to Zephyr. "You can jump to the ground, and without your weight, I'll rise up, with the bag."

Good idea, Holly thought. "Yes, do that!"

Zephyr stuck his neck farther out of his shell and twisted until he could hook the strap of the bag around one of the gecko's feet. Leaf's toes jutted out of his balloon body. They curled around the strap.

"Got it," Leaf said. "Ready?"

Zephyr eyed the ground below. "Maybe over the moss —"

Leaf let go, and Zephyr tucked his head, arms, and legs into his shell. He landed on dirt and slid downhill, faster and faster, spinning as he slid.

"Zephyr!" Holly called after him.

She watched him slide directly into a tangle of brambles. The thin branches of the bushes snapped as he plowed through them, but they slowed him. He stuck his legs and arms out, and that was enough to stop his slide.

"I'm okay!" he called.

Leaf, with the bag, was floating high above, out of reach. He drifted with the sun behind him, ringing the globular gecko in a golden glow.

"Keep floating!" Holly yelled. "Get to safety!"

"I'm sorry, Zephyr and Holly." Leaf began to deflate.

"What are you doing?" Holly called, a note of panic in her voice.

Charlie chuckled softly.

"I know you don't understand," Leaf said, "but I don't want to be this way anymore. It's too hard." He swam his legs through the air, propelling himself toward the beaver.

Zephyr stared up. "Leaf?"

Holly began to grasp what Leaf was saying. "Please don't give Charlie the bag."

But he sank lower and lower.

"I'll grab it!" Zephyr cried.

As he hurried over a rock, a rose hit him.

Then a lily. A daisy. A tulip . . .

Like a waterfall, a torrent of conjured blossoms poured over the turtle, knocking him onto the back of his shell. His legs waved helplessly in the air.

Holly and Periwinkle rushed down from their tree to help him. Petals cascaded over them, falling faster and faster, obscuring the sky. They batted and clawed their way through the flowers. Reaching Zephyr, they righted him.

But by the time he'd zoomed out of the pile of blossoms and Holly and Periwinkle had cleared enough away to see the sky again, Leaf and Charlie were gone.

Chapter Eighteen

With her tail, Holly dusted rose petals off Zephyr's shell. "We need a plan."

"I'll run really fast," Zephyr said.

He'd crash into pine trees if he tried that here. The forest was too thick. But aside from that, they had other problems. "What are you going to do if we catch them? Fight our friends? Fight your best friend?"

"Well, no, of course not," Zephyr said. "But we know exactly where they're going. I can beat them there, and we can stop them."

"Stop them how?" Holly asked. She knew how Zephyr felt. She too wanted to race after them and "stop them." But it was the specifics that tripped her up. It sounded all great and brave to say they'd "stop them," but what exactly did that mean? Capture Charlie somehow? And then what?

"Take the ingredients," Zephyr said. "And this time, don't give them to Leaf!"

Holly winced. She knew how close Zephyr and Leaf were, and she knew how it felt when a friend betrayed you. It had felt as if she were standing on a branch that had been chewed through. "I'm sorry about Leaf."

Zephyr pulled his head into his shell. "I should have seen it. He never wanted his magic."

"So, let me get this straight," Periwinkle said. "Charlie wants to steal our magic, which makes him a thief, and Leaf decided to help him? Even though Charlie's a thief?" Perched halfway up a tree, her paws tight around a branch, the lemur was looking at them with enormous eyes.

"Yes," Holly said.

"I thought I was doing a good thing by helping him. You all greeted him like a returning hero. I thought if I helped him, everyone would like me."

"None of us knew," Holly said. "Now we have to figure out what to do about it —"

From above, a friendly voice called, "Hello!"

Holly looked up and saw Gus circle above them and then land in a pine tree. "Gus!" She'd never been so happy to see someone. After Charlie's betrayal . . . after Leaf's . . . she needed her true friend, even though he was too late to help.

"And me!" Bluebell called as he hopped up the slope.

"Sorry," Gus said. "We would have been here faster if *someone* hadn't lost his hat and demanded I chase it down."

"It was a wide-brimmed bonnet," Bluebell said. "You blame me for a gust of wind?"

"I do blame you. You could have tied it on." Sailing down from the tree, Gus landed on the rocky mountainside. He folded his wings against his sides.

Holly scampered toward them. "Very, very glad to see you two."

Gus surveyed the mountain slope. "What did we miss?"

Glancing around with fresh eyes, Holly thought it looked rather like a garden had vomited five seasons' worth of flowers. The ground was littered with blossoms. Even after seeing Charlie with the rats at the crater, she hadn't guessed he was capable of summoning so many so quickly. He didn't have to steal others' magic to be powerful. He was powerful already.

His head still within his shell, Zephyr said in a muffled voice, "It's too much to explain."

Holly summarized: "Periwinkle found the crystal, Zephyr stole it, Leaf stole it back, and now Leaf and Charlie are on the way to Cloud Mountain so that Charlie can steal all our magic for himself."

"Okay, maybe it's not too much to explain," Zephyr said, still muffled.

Gus spread his wings. "So why aren't we racing to Cloud Mountain? We don't know whether Clover, Pepper, and Tangerine have made it there yet. The trail up the mountain could be unguarded."

"We're going," Holly said, "but we need a plan." She wished there were a way to warn the others. They'd said they'd guard the trail, just in case, but they wouldn't know that Charlie had all the ingredients or that Leaf had joined him. She also didn't know how they'd stop Charlie once they reached the Moon Mirror.

Zephyr stuck his head back out. "It's simple: we sneak up on them, I zip in and steal the ingredients, and then we cast the real spell — the original one to fix the pool."

"And if we fail in this endeavor, we destroy as many of the ingredients as we can," Bluebell said. He thumped his hind paws for emphasis.

"I can help with that!" Periwinkle said. "Crush the flower, smash the herb, crack the crystal, eat the desert fruit, and . . . I don't know what you do to destroy a meteorite."

"Throw it really far away?" Zephyr suggested.

Holly wished they had a better plan. Grabbing the ingredients hadn't worked this time, but what else could they do? They had to try. "We can figure out the details later. Let's just get to Cloud Mountain, before it's too late."

All of them nodded in agreement.

✦

The problem was how to get all five of them there quickly.

Holly climbed up onto a rock and saw the train in the distance, its smoke curling up toward the clouds. Chances were very good that Charlie and Leaf were on it. "Zephyr . . ."

The turtle jumped to his feet. "Ready for another run!"

Gus shook out his wings. "I haven't flown this much in . . . well, ever. I've never flown this much. You go ahead. I'll rest a bit and then catch up, if I can."

"Nay," Bluebell said, "We must stick together! United, we will be a force that cannot be denied!"

Holly eyed Zephyr's shell. It had fit her and Leaf, but the gecko was significantly smaller. She didn't think she, Bluebell, Periwinkle, *and* Gus could fit. If only there were a way to make his shell bigger . . .

Or . . .

"What if you pulled us?" Holly suggested. He often said he was both fast *and* strong. She wondered how strong he truly was. Obsessed with his speed, he'd never fully tested his strength.

"I could do that. Maybe?" He looked at them dubiously. "I don't know that it would be comfortable. You'd be bounced over dirt and rocks and everything."

She'd seen horses and oxen pull carts and had even heard of dogs pulling sleds over ice. She scanned the mountainside for anything that could work as a sled. Maybe a log? A few logs strapped together like a raft? "If only we had something you could pull us on . . ."

Periwinkle piped up. "How about a hat?"

Everyone looked at Bluebell's wide-brimmed hat. He struck several poses, showing off his hat from multiple angles. He flopped his ears forward and back, and the ribbons fluttered in the breeze.

"Bluebell, how large and sturdy can you make your hat?" Holly asked.

"I can make it magnificent!" He concentrated, and a puff of pink smoke poofed up as his hat transformed into an even wider-brimmed hat.

"Large enough to hold the four of us?"

Another puff of pink, and an improbably wide hat appeared on his head, the brim dipping down to touch the ground. "So much magnificence, yes?"

"Absolutely. Can you make it sturdier?" A felt hat would tear on any rocks and branches Zephyr dragged it over. "How about metal? Like when you changed your hat into a helmet?"

A third puff, and the rabbit disappeared beneath an enormous, metal, very wide-brimmed hat. Pink smoke dispersed into the air as they all admired the helmet sled.

I think that will work, Holly thought. "Can you add ribbons?"

A fourth puff, and bright pink ribbons unfurled from either side. "Strong ribbons?"

They thickened into rope, still pink.

Bluebell wiggled out from under the helmet and flopped over the rocks dramatically. "I must rest. With great artistry comes great exhaustion." He immediately began to make snoring noises.

Periwinkle peered at him. "He's faking it." She poked him with a long finger, and he rolled onto his side.

Zephyr zipped in a circle around him before bumping into a blueberry bush. "Don't rest, you ham! We have to go! We can't waste any more time!"

Feigning exhaustion, Bluebell crawled onto the hat and continued fake snoring as loud as a train, as if to emphasize the cost of his "artistry." Holly, Gus, and Periwinkle climbed on board beside him. Zephyr took two of the pink ropes in his mouth. Holly held the other ends as if they were reins. *This could work*, she thought.

Squirrels had very fast reflexes. All Zephyr would have to do was turn when she pulled the ribbons. He wouldn't have to make the snap judgments of when and which way to turn; she'd do that part for him. "You run," she told Zephyr. "I'll steer you."

"Mmmrrr-fect," he said around the ropes in his mouth.

"Bluebell, quit playing and hold on," Holly told the rabbit. Gus and Periwinkle were already holding on to ropes, braced for the turtle to begin his run.

With an exaggerated yawn, Bluebell blinked his eyes open. "The squirrel wakes me with dulcet tones — Ahhh!" He grabbed on to a pink rope as Zephyr spurted ahead.

The hat bounced over the rocks, and Holly concentrated on steering. She kept her eyes fixed on the tree trunks. A tug on the left rope pulled Zephyr to the left. She experimented with how hard she had to pull — he zigzagged between the trees as she got the feel for how to help him steer.

Hind paws spread wide, she used her tail to keep herself steady. They raced down the mountain, over the hills, and onto farmland — dodging trees, rocks, fallen logs, placid cows, and very startled sheep.

"Woo-hoo!" Bluebell cried, fully awake.

Holly concentrated on steering the speeding turtle down a road, passing a steam-powered car and a cart pulled by a horse.

"This is amazing!" Bluebell cried, waving at the humans as they careened by.

The humans, confused but polite, waved back.

Holly steered them through a town, zipping by pedestrians, vehicles, and a barking dog who demanded to know what they were doing and was left unsatisfied when they zoomed past without pausing to explain.

Only when Zephyr began to slow did they stop and rest. They drank from a stream, and Holly gathered a few mushrooms for the turtle to eat. Then they continued on.

"You know, I think this is helping," Zephyr said. "Seeing when you tell me to turn . . . I think I'm getting a better feel for the timing."

"Do you want to try steering yourself?" Holly asked.

"No!" Bluebell said loudly.

"Not yet," Zephyr said. "But . . . I think, yes, someday."

They kept going until nightfall. Then they tumbled off the hat, exhausted, and slept in the shadow of a hay bale. Holly woke at dawn, afraid that Charlie wouldn't have stopped, that he'd somehow already reached the pool and cast his spell. She concentrated and was relieved when a cupcake appeared in her hand.

Gus, waking, asked, "Everything okay?"

"Fine," she said, offering the cupcake to Periwinkle, who ate it in three gulps. "He hasn't cast his spell yet."

Shaking out his wings, Gus preened his feathers. "I thought you didn't care whether you had your magic. You always said it was a ridiculous power for a squirrel." Quickly, he added, "Not that I agree."

"I thought I didn't care either, but it's a part of me," Holly said.

"And . . . maybe I just hadn't found the best way to use it." Her magic had been useful with the seagulls and had helped guide them out of the caves.

Gus stretched out his wings. "We'll get there in time, and we'll stop him."

"I hope so."

She'd been so dejected when she'd first come to the Shelter for Rejected Familiars. But since then . . . It had been a while since she'd felt like a failure, she realized. Ever since Periwinkle's arrival . . . No, before that. Ever since Gus had arrived and they'd become friends, she'd focused on making the shelter a true home for herself and the others. *That* had become her purpose.

When she'd lost her dream of becoming a familiar, the shelter had given her a new path. She just hadn't known until now that "rejected familiar" was a thing she could *want* to be — and would miss if it were taken away from her.

Maybe her life hadn't turned out the way she'd thought it would, but she'd made a new life out of the remnants of her old dreams, and she wasn't ready to lose that. She'd become a shelterling, and now she'd learned she could even go on adventures, though the wizards had told her that someone like her couldn't. *Maybe*, she thought, *the wizards were wrong about me.*

And maybe I was wrong about them. She hadn't needed a wizard to make the shelter a better place or to help improve her friends' lives.

She prodded the turtle with her paw. "Zephyr, are you awake?"

"Mrr-hmmrph."

"Can you run again?"

He hopped to his feet. "Just try to stop me!"

Holly, Gus, Periwinkle, and Bluebell climbed onto the hat again and held on, and, with Holly at the reins, Zephyr ran at top speed toward Cloud Mountain.

Chapter Nineteen

They reached Cloud Mountain at noon.

It matched Holly's memory: thick with evergreen, maple, and birch trees. It was awash in deep summer green, a beautiful, tempting green that made the mountain look as if it welcomed every creature who wanted to live in its nooks and crannies. She could hear the birds in the trees, calling to one another, staking out their territories and reporting on the presence of fresh berries. It smelled wonderful too, full of pine and rich earth. She remembered how the scent had buoyed her on the climb up the mountain — and how it had surrounded her on the way down. She'd been so happy then, until the wizards had proclaimed that her magic was small and useless . . . that *she* was small and useless.

She'd forgotten how happy she'd felt, but it all came back with the scent.

As they sped toward the foot of the mountain, Holly kept checking to make sure she could still conjure pastries. So far so good. It looked as if they'd made it to the mountain before Charlie and Leaf. Certainly the beaver and gecko couldn't have matched Zephyr's speed, especially now that he wasn't crashing as much, but it was possible they hadn't had to stop for the night to sleep. And if they'd taken another train, that could have cut their travel time significantly.

"Ready to climb?" Holly asked. Over the years, animals seeking the Moon Mirror had worn a trail up the forested slope. The trailhead was marked by a pile of stones, as well as pine cones and acorn caps, all left by prior creatures who'd wanted magic too.

Zephyr, panting, said, "Just . . . let me rest a minute." He flopped down, legs spread out, next to the marker.

"Of course," Holly said. "As long as you need." *So long as it's not very long*, she added silently. She wished she knew exactly where Charlie was and where the other shelterlings were. They'd set out from the shelter at approximately the same time as —

Bluebell shrunk his hat and waved it in the air. "Hello, friends!"

Holly looked up to see a welcome sight above them on the trail: the other shelterlings! A bright-purple porcupine rode on the back of a cow, while a flamingo flew beside them.

"We knew you'd make it!" Pepper said.

"No, we didn't," Tangerine said. "At least not until Clover rhymed."

"I told them you wouldn't come," Clover said modestly. "Your task was already done. It wasn't a perfect rhyme, but at least it was relevant."

Holly jumped to ask, "Charlie — is he here? Have you seen him?"

"Not a tuft of fur or a hint of tail," Tangerine said. "And we've been guarding the trail nonstop for a day."

We're not too late, she thought with relief.

For the first time since she'd left the shelter, she felt as if they had a real chance. All of them were here, and Charlie hadn't yet cast his spell. "Do you still have the spell?" she asked the porcupine.

He changed from purple back to his usual brown, and the paper the spell was written on stood out against the darker color of his quills. "Don't touch," he warned her. "I don't want to accidentally stick you." He then disguised it again, turning himself and the paper back to brilliant purple.

"Good," she said.

This wasn't over yet.

Her friends were looking at her, as if waiting for her to tell them what to do.

"Charlie is on his way, and he has all seven ingredients, but we have each other," Holly said. "And while our powers may not be what we expected . . . we are powerful. We've proved it over the last few days. Look at all we've done!"

She saw nods from her friends, and heard them echo her, as if tasting the word "powerful." It tasted as sweet and satisfying as fresh honeycomb. Clover straightened, her big eyes clear. Bluebell transformed his hat into an officer's cap.

"Charlie said he was able to trick us because we *wanted* to be tricked," Holly said. "He thinks we're pathetic and useless. But I say we show him that it's not up to him to say who we are or how we feel or what we can do. *We* say who we are!"

This time, the shelterlings cheered.

"Now let's defend our magic!" Gus shouted.

Leading the way, Holly scampered up the trail. The owl and the flamingo flew above her, while the porcupine waddled beside her. Zephyr sped and then crashed, of course, while Clover the cow ambled along. Tangerine switched between various shades of red as he waddled past the greenery. Bluebell changed his hat into a pith helmet as he hopped between the trees, and Periwinkle jumped from branch to branch.

Her friends chattered as they climbed, swapping tales of their journey and sharing their shock over Leaf's behavior, but Holly didn't listen. She was focused on the top of the mountain. She caught glimpses of it between the trees, wreathed in clouds to match its name, and she saw the hint of pine trees as they appeared and disappeared within the mist. As they climbed higher, her friends quieted, and all she heard was the whisper of wind.

And then they were there.

She lifted a branch from a raspberry bush, ducked under the leaves, and saw it. Sheltered by a semicircle of boulders, the pool lay in the shadows. It was perfectly round. White pebbles circled it, and the water gave off a pale blue glow. It looked as if the moon were sleeping, cradled by the mountain.

The Moon Mirror, she thought.

Hushed, the shelterlings approached the edge. Holly inched closer to the pool and looked at her reflection.

A squirrel stared back at her: ordinary, with gray fur, black eyes and whiskers, and tufted ears, no different from any other squirrel in the forest she'd come from.

Gus broke the silence. "He's not here yet."

"Holly, what do we do?" Periwinkle asked.

"I'm ready," Zephyr said. "Just tell me when he's here, and I'll zip forward and grab his bag."

"Surround the Moon Mirror," Holly ordered. "And watch for Charlie."

As the others circled the pool, jostling for a position, Holly whispered to Gus, "I wish we had a better plan than just 'grab the bag.' Zephyr tried to grab the bag before, and it didn't work."

"Last time, you couldn't have predicted Leaf. That won't happen again."

He was right. Still . . .

Worrying, Holly squeezed her tail as she watched the misty woods. Charlie could come at any time. She didn't know how long they'd have to wait —

A single rose tumbled off one of the boulders and landed in the pool.

Everyone stared at it for a moment as it floated, petals perfectly open, in the glowing water. And then Holly shook herself and shouted, "He's here!"

"Where?" Pepper asked, raising her neck up to look in every direction.

"In the woods!" Gus called. "I see movement!" He flew low toward the trees. The others followed him, hurrying toward the trail. Holly couldn't see anything —

Wait, there!

Leaf floated, balloon-like, between the trees.

Zephyr called, "Leaf! Join us!"

"Where's Charlie?" Periwinkle asked.

Stopping at the edge of the woods in front of the start of the trail, the shelterlings peered into the mist. *He's coming*, Holly thought. She was sure of it. Any second now.

She felt a breeze tickle her tail.

She twitched it, then glanced over her shoulder. She let out a squeak of alarm.

Roses were tumbling out of the woods on either side of the Moon Mirror, bursting into existence so quickly that they heaped on top of one another. Sprigs of blackberry bushes, with their fragile white flowers and wicked thorns, joined them. Crown-of-thorns flowers. Hawthorn branches. And springs of holly, with their pointed leaves. Piles of every kind of thorny and sharp flower grew higher and higher, halfway between the shelterlings and the pool.

"He's making a wall!" Holly cried.

He was trying to keep them from the Moon Mirror. She thought of the single rose that had tumbled off the boulder behind the pool. He could already be beyond his barricade of thorns. All he'd been waiting for was Leaf to draw the shelterlings far enough away.

And we fell for it, she thought.

"Climb on," Gus told Holly.

She scrambled onto the owl's back. The others . . . "Zephyr, bash through! Make a path!" The thorns wouldn't hurt his shell. He could plow through them.

Tucking his head into his shell, Zephyr revved up his feet

and rammed into the wall of thorny flowers. Branches and stems snapped from the force of his impact. Reversing, he retreated and then bashed them again.

On Gus's back, Holly flew over the barricade. He glided down to land beside the Moon Mirror. Carrying Tangerine, Pepper landed beside them. She knelt, and the porcupine climbed off.

Looking in every direction, Holly didn't see Charlie, either by the water or in the nearby woods. He was still generating thorny blossoms from his hiding place.

It's not too late, Holly thought. *We can stop him.*

After all, he wasn't the only one with magic.

Concentrating, Holly spread her paws and began conjuring pastries, the largest she'd ever created: cinnamon rolls several times the size of her head, éclairs twice as long as her body, croissants that were too plump for her to wrap her arms around.

Two can play at this game, she thought grimly. All they had to do was keep Charlie away from the Moon Mirror. The semicircle of boulders blocked access from the back and the sides. If they could prevent him from drawing close enough to the front of the pool to cast his spell, then they could figure out their next step.

Behind her, Zephyr burst through the thorns. Clover stomped through behind him, grinding the remaining thorny branches into the ground. Periwinkle and Bluebell followed.

"Everyone with a free paw," Holly called to them, "use the pastries to build a wall in front of the pool. Keep Charlie away from its edge!" Flaky pastry tumbled off her paws faster and faster. She concentrated on making each one as large as possible.

Periwinkle took the lead, hurrying to the Moon Mirror and building a wall of baked goods like a dam in front of it, and the others quickly joined her, using mud, jelly, and cream filling as mortar. Together they built the barricade higher and higher, pastry by pastry. Gus said to Holly, "You're doing great. Keep it up."

So far so good. The wall was rising higher, and she hadn't seen either Charlie or Leaf. Everyone was working together to build the barricade.

Gus flew up onto the branch of a pine tree. "We can do this, everyone! All of us combined can keep him from ever reaching the pool. He only has flower power. What can he do against — oh. Uh, Holly?"

Holly looked where Gus was staring. Above the Moon Mirror, on one of the boulders, Charlie stood on his hind legs and held a crystal in one paw and a chunk of meteorite in the other.

And she remembered what else Saffron had said: how the spell needed the ingredients because the ingredients amplified magic. *All magic?* she wondered. *Including Charlie's?*

CHAPTER TWENTY

Holly called up to Charlie, "We won't let you steal our magic."

"Oh, Holly, do you really think you can stop me? This is truly for the best," Charlie said.

"For you, but not for us," Holly said.

"For the world!" He thumped the ground with his tail for emphasis. "Who wants a bunch of useless shelterlings when you can have one ultrapowerful beaver?"

His words hurt, but it was already clear how he saw them. "You aren't doing this for the world *or* for us," Holly said. Maybe once, he'd cared about the shelterlings, but he'd rejected the kind and patient Charlie that she'd loved in favor of becoming . . . what had he called it? Oh yes: a legendary familiar who needed no wizard.

Or maybe he'd never really cared about them at all. Perhaps this was what he'd always wanted, and he'd just been biding his time until he could put his plan into action. He'd always referred to the shelterlings as mistakes and failures; she hadn't realized how deeply that went. She thought of how he'd left the shelter with only a vague explanation, and how he'd behaved since he'd returned —

his secrecy and his displays of temper. All the clues had been there. She simply hadn't wanted to see it.

She'd been so wrong about him.

Just as wrong as he was about them.

Neither Charlie nor the wizards had seen the shelterlings as they truly were.

"Yeah, it's our magic, not yours," Periwinkle said. "You're just a thief! I should know." She shot a look at Bluebell, who nodded graciously at her.

The shelterlings shuffled closer together.

"Keep guarding the Moon Mirror," Holly told them. "He needs to be near it for the spell to work." If he couldn't lay the ingredients at the edge of the water, he couldn't cast the spell on them. Saffron had been very clear about that. The conditions of the original spell had to be replicated for Charlie's amended spell to work. She scampered up the rock toward Charlie and halted a few feet away. She smelled the scent of roses wafting off him.

"Everyone, back away from the Moon Mirror," Charlie said. "No harm will come to you if you don't stand in my way. You have my word."

"Or what?" Holly asked him. "Can't you see that doing this *will* harm us?"

"Nonsense," Charlie snapped. "Whether you believe in my good intentions or not, this *is* the way for all of us to be happy. I'm correcting mistakes that were made."

"We're not mistakes," Holly said.

As soon as the words were out of her mouth, she felt as though a weight had lifted from on top of her tail. She repeated it: "We're not mistakes. And you don't get to say who or what we are. No one does."

Charlie snorted. "The wizards disagree."

"I'm not friends with any wizards," Gus said, "and I don't care what they think."

"You cared when they didn't make you a familiar," Charlie said. "All of you did. Holly, remember when you first arrived at the shelter? You cried on my shoulder. Sloppy tears that clumped my fur, and I cried with you."

Leaf popped up behind Charlie, his head visible over the curve of the boulder. "Let him cast the spell! Please! We can be free of failed magic — magic that has never led to anything good!"

Zephyr protested, "It led to us! You and me, Leaf. We would never have met if it weren't for the water of the Moon Mirror." He zipped around the pool and bumped into the trunk of the pine tree where Gus was perched. Startled, the owl took flight and sailed down to land next to Holly.

"Same with all of us," Holly said, looking at Gus. If not for drinking from the Moon Mirror, they never would have ended up at the shelter together, and she'd have missed out on her best friend. "Because of the Moon Mirror, we all have each other. Because of the choice we each made, we have a home, together."

Charlie scoffed, "The shelter is not a home."

"Of course it is," Holly said. "People living together who love one another — that's what home is." She tried to find the words she'd failed to find before. "We all came here, to Cloud Mountain to drink from the Moon Mirror, because we wanted to walk a different path. And that's exactly what we did. We changed ourselves and our future."

"Sure, we became failures," Charlie said.

Clover spoke up. "I'm not a failure."

"You?" Charlie sputtered. "You're one of the worst failures of all! Look at your power of prophecy. You have to play word-association games to even come up with a relevant prediction. And then every word you speak is wrong!"

"Always and reliably wrong," Clover agreed, "which makes me as good as right. And the word games work — I've been able to improve. In fact, I'll prophesize right now: I predict you will understand and will soon leave this peak, and we will have the peace we seek." And then her head drooped low, as she realized what her prophecy meant. "Oh dear."

Oh dear indeed, Holly thought. Her friends whispered worriedly to one another. Charlie wasn't going to understand or leave anytime soon. Anxiously, Zephyr zigzagged in front of the pond and ricocheted off a rock.

"You see our quirks as weaknesses," Holly said. "But you're wrong. You see weaknesses, but I see strengths!"

"My 'quirk' isn't a strength," Leaf said. "You can conjure pastries whenever you want. You always have control of your power. If there's so much as a stiff breeze, I'm in danger of floating away."

Before she could reply, the turtle was already shouting back at his friend. "You think *I* don't understand what it's like to have a power that's hard to use?" Zephyr spun in a circle from frustration. "How many times have I bashed into the furniture in the shelter? How many bushes and trees and —"

"And don't you wish you were done with all of it?" Leaf asked.

"Zephyr, tell Leaf how many times we crashed on the way here," Holly said.

Leaf scoffed. "Over and over. I've traveled with you. I know —"

Zephyr cut him off. "Zero. Can you guess why? Bluebell transformed his hat into a sled, and Holly steered me with ribbons. Together, we found a new way to control and use my magic."

Staring, Leaf said, "You didn't crash once?"

"Not once," Zephyr said. *"That's* what we need to do with you and your magic: find a way to work with it. Yes, you float, but what if a friend — your best friend, me — helped guide you? And what if you helped guide me? If we attached a ribbon between us, you could steer me wherever you wanted to go. It could work! If only you'd try!"

Periwinkle piped up. "I have ribbons in my room. You can have some."

"And I can conjure more," Bluebell offered. "Just say the word."

"I . . . I don't know," Leaf said.

Focusing again on Charlie, Holly said, "You see? We've been looking at ourselves all wrong. Our quirky magic doesn't make us failures. It makes us powerful. And once we can see that, then we can do and be anything!"

Her words rang out across the peak, and everyone stared at

Charlie, waiting for him to speak. Holly held her breath. Surely he'd give up now that he saw they were united against him.

Charlie placed the crystal and meteorite on the ground, and then he clapped. Slowly.

Clap.

Clap.

Clap.

"Beautiful words, Holly," Charlie said. "Really, all of you, so inspiring."

There was a note in his voice, a dryness that she didn't like.

"I'm moved. Truly, I am, and so proud of you for how far you've come and how much you've grown," Charlie said. And then he added: "But I still want your magic."

✦

Quickly, before any of them could react, Charlie scooped up the crystal and meteorite again, and he conjured a stream of long-stemmed roses into the air faster than she'd ever seen him conjure before.

The roses rocketed like arrows toward the shelterlings.

Leaf cried, "What are you doing? Don't hurt them!"

"Scatter!" Holly shouted.

Everyone ran, hopped, and flew from the barrage of blooms.

Gus transformed into stone, shielding Holly, Tangerine, and Blue-bell, and the thorny blossoms smacked into his granite feathers. Zephyr pulled his head and legs into his shell.

Clover mooed. "Behind me!"

Pepper and Periwinkle ducked behind the cow.

And then, just as suddenly as the barrage started, it stopped. Holly peeked out around Gus in time to see Charlie conjure yet another flower. This time, though, the blossom was utterly gigantic, with petals that were larger than Clover. She didn't know how such a massive flower was possible unless . . . *It must be the ingredients*, she thought. They were enhancing his power. Or else he'd *really* been practicing.

"Stop him!" Holly yelled.

Yelling and squawking and howling, they ran and flew toward the beaver.

And another flower materialized on top of them, burying them in soft pinkness. He conjured giant flower after giant flower. The sky disappeared, swaddled in pink. Her friends disappeared.

Muffled, from beyond the blossoms, she heard Leaf call, "Charlie, no more! You're taking it too far!"

Holly reached out her paws, but all she felt were petals. A burst of panic welled up. What if she couldn't find her friends in time? What if they were lost — *lost!* She latched onto the word. "Periwinkle, can you find everyone?"

The lemur's voice sounded faraway. "I can try!"

Holly shoved through the petals. Every petal she pushed aside revealed yet another layer of pink. She clawed at them with panic rising through her. The overwhelming floral scent filled her skull, and she coughed.

She heard Zephyr's panicky voice. "I can't see which way to run! Where's Charlie?"

Charlie was out there, maybe casting his spell already. *They had to get free!* "Periwinkle, find Zephyr!" She clawed at a pink petal, and a bird squawked. "Pepper! I'm sorry!" All pink, the flamingo had blended in. "Are you all right?"

"A few feathers short, but I'm okay." She stabbed at a petal with her beak.

An idea occurred to Holly. "Can you raise me up?" The flamingo's power was to extend her standing leg. Maybe on Pepper's back, she'd be able to see over the flowers.

"Climb on."

Holly scrambled up the flamingo's wing onto her back. "Ready!"

The flamingo's left leg stretched and stretched, and Holly shot higher through the petals. She squeezed her eyes shut as she and Pepper tore through the flowers. At last, she felt sunlight on her fur. She opened her eyes.

Clear of the flowers, Holly peered down at the pool.

Charlie had laid the ingredients at the water's edge.

Oh no! she thought. All their efforts, and he'd still reached the Moon Mirror. He had everything he needed to cast the spell right now. "We have to stop him!"

Lifting her elongated leg, Pepper flapped toward the water. As she approached, Charlie slammed his broad tail down over the ingredients, protecting them. He then launched a barrage of flying roses, hurling them at the flamingo.

"Watch out!" Holly cried.

Pepper retreated, flapping her wings. "I'm sorry, Holly! I can't get close!"

She heard Charlie chant, syllables from the spell: "Elt eth igmac wrog . . ." And Holly felt prickles all over her fur. This was it. He was doing it!

Concentrating, Holly conjured pastries, one for each paw. She threw them as hard as she could at the beaver, but she was too far away. They splatted harmlessly around him.

Charlie laughed as a macaroon landed in the water with a splash. "You think you're powerful? You're useless. I'll show you power!"

He continued the spell. "Elt eth werop lifl . . ."

"What do we do?" Pepper asked.

"Lower me down," Holly instructed. "We need everybody."

As they descended into the petals, she heard her friends scrambling beneath them.

"Clover," Holly called, "are we too late?"

The cow's voice drifted up, mournful. "The spell has been cast; our time is past."

It's not over yet, Holly thought. They had to get out of the blossoms and get Charlie away from the ingredients. She had ideas on how to do both. "Zephyr, crash through as many petals as fast as you can. Don't worry about which direction to run. Just crush them. Gus, turn to stone — whoever is near him, Periwinkle or Bluebell, roll him through the flowers. Mow them down! Clover, smash them with your hooves!"

She heard her friends, even though she couldn't see them, attacking the petals with renewed gusto. Zephyr bashed through blossoms, creating a flurry of ripped petals. Clover stomped like a one-cow stampede.

"Tangerine? Tangerine, where are you?" She peered through the pinkness and saw a hint of brilliant green. There he was! As Gus and Zephyr and the others destroyed the petals around her, she waded through the debris toward the bright green porcupine.

"We aren't useless," Holly said, both to herself and to Tangerine. "We just have to work with what we have."

"What do you need me to do?" Tangerine asked.

"We have to get Charlie away from the ingredients," she said. "I need you to climb on Pepper's back and ready your quills. I know you don't like to use them, but — "

"I'll do it," he said without any hesitation.

Pepper lowered her wing, and the porcupine climbed up onto her back. At Holly's command, she grew her leg and raised Tangerine into the air.

As soon as they cleared the flower carnage, the porcupine leaped from the flamingo's back. Curling into a ball in midair, he hurtled toward Charlie, quills first. He was bright red against the blue sky.

Intent on his spell, Charlie didn't see him until a few seconds before impact. He twisted away, but he wasn't fast enough. Tangerine slammed into the beaver's shoulder. "Yow!" Charlie cried.

The porcupine scampered down the beaver's back, leaving multiple quills behind, and Bluebell sprang into action. "Oh, glorious hat for me!" he cried as he transformed his hat into a bowler embellished with ostrich plumes and other feathers.

He flung it at Charlie.

Distracted by the quills, Charlie didn't see it coming. The rabbit's hat hit the beaver full in the chest, and the feathers thwacked his face. Before he could recover, a cream-filled puff pastry, thrown by Holly, splattered all over him, followed by a jelly donut. Stumbling backwards, he wiped the cream and jelly out of his eyes . . .

. . . and as he reeled from the barrage of quills, hat, and pastries, he shifted his tail, exposing the ingredients.

"Now!" Holly cried. "Get the ingredients!"

Everyone charged forward on paws, hooves, and wings as Charlie shouted, "Elt it meco ot em nad elt ti eb niem! Let it be as I have willed!" He then let out a crowing laugh. "You're too late! It's done!"

Stopping, all the shelterlings stared at the moonlike water.

He'd finished casting the spell.

CHAPTER TWENTY-ONE

Charlie, chuckling to himself, didn't resist as Holly grabbed the crystal and meteorite out of his paws, Zephyr darted in to snap up the magic flower by the stem, Gus grabbed the herb in his talons, and Periwinkle scooped up the pearl.

Charlie merely smiled.

All of them waited for the Moon Mirror to steal their magic.

But Holly didn't feel anything. The water in the pool calmly reflected the clouds overhead. After a minute, Holly concentrated — and a blueberry muffin popped into her paws.

Huh, she thought. *That's unexpected.*

Around them, the others experimented too. Gus did a wing-stand and turned to granite and back to feathers. Bluebell changed his hat into a top hat. Zephyr sped until he bumped into a tree.

"What?" said Charlie. "It didn't work? But . . . but I don't understand!" He sputtered. "I had all the ingredients! You were fools enough to gather them, and the others held them. I cast the spell, as the animals did so long ago. I did it all exactly right — exactly the same! — but with only a few words changed, to alter the effects. It should have worked! I did everything right!"

Standing in front of a leaf, Tangerine changed his quills to bright purple. "Apparently not."

Holly crossed to the Moon Mirror and stared at her reflection. *Charlie said he'd cast the spell exactly as the animals long ago, so why . . .* "You didn't do it the same as they did," she said as the answer dawned on her. "You cast it by yourself. Alone. It was a group of animals, working together, who found the ingredients *and* cast the original spell."

Charlie's jaw dropped.

It was only a guess, but it felt right. If he had to re-create the circumstances of the first spell in order to cast it, then he needed a group of friends helping him. He didn't have that.

"You chose to turn on your friends, instead of working with them," Gus said to Charlie. "That's why you failed. And that's why you should leave." He spread his wings wide. One by one, the others came to stand on either side of him, Holly joining him first, then Periwinkle, then Clover, then Bluebell with his hat, Pepper, Tangerine, and Zephyr. Only Leaf hung back, as if unsure where he belonged anymore. Clover scraped the ground with her front hoof. "If you conjure a single flower, you'll learn how hard a cow can kick." She paused and added, "That's fact, not prophecy."

Charlie opened his mouth to argue.

Holly cut him off. "Not another word."

"My dear Holly —"

Tangerine rattled his remaining quills. "She said not another word. It's over."

"You can't have defeated me!" Charlie said. "You're *shelter-lings!*"

"Yes, we are," Periwinkle said proudly. "And you aren't one of us anymore."

He sputtered as if he'd run out of words. With one final glare at all of them, Charlie fled, rushing down the mountain with his tail thumping behind him and his shoulder covered in porcupine quills.

Zephyr looked at Holly questioningly. "Let him go," she said. "He can't hurt us."

"We did it!" Gus cheered.

Pepper whooped and flew in a celebratory circle, while Blue-bell tossed his hat in the air. Periwinkle caught the hat and handed it back to him. He thanked her and then transformed his hat into a festive fruit-laden bonnet.

"But what did he do to the Moon Mirror?" Zephyr worried. "He still cast a spell, even if it didn't work the way he wanted it to."

All of them hurried back to the water. It looked okay, but how could they be sure? What if Charlie's altered spell had messed up its magic in some way they couldn't see? What if he'd broken the very thing they'd come here to fix?

"Whatever Charlie did with his spell, we can undo it," Gus said stoutly. "We have the original spell and all the ingredients."

He's right, she thought. "Come on, everyone. Let's finish this together."

They laid the ingredients at the edge of the water.

Tangerine trotted forward, and Holly plucked the paper with the spell off his quills. Smoothing the page with the pads of her paws, she began to carefully pronounce the original glyphs, without any of Charlie's alterations. "Elt eth igmac wrog . . ."

In unison, the others repeated: "Elt eth igmac wrog."

The magic items began to glow — the flower green, the herb orange, the crystal blue, the meteorite purple, the volcanic rock yellow, the desert fruit red . . . As the creatures continued to chant, the ingredients glowed brighter.

It's working! Holly thought.

Pressing closer to one another and to the Moon Mirror, they continued. "Elt ti wolf otni eth retaw . . ." The glow brightened until they were all tinted green, orange, blue, and purple, and the light shot straight up into the sky, changing the clouds into a rainbow of colors.

"Keep going," Zephyr cried to Holly.

She kept reciting the spell, and her friends echoed her. Inching closer, Leaf chimed in with them.

The pool began to glow, a sparkling blue. Shimmering light chased over the surface, and the water swirled like a whirlpool.

At last they reached the end of the spell: "Let it be as it will be!"

Light flashed and then rolled in a wave of rainbows over them and down the mountain, and it kept going, spilling across the land as far as they could see. Holly inched nearer to the edge of the pool. The rainbow glow was beginning to fade. She looked into the smooth surface. It reflected her, haloed in colors.

"It's beautiful," Gus said.

"It is," Holly said.

Holly put her paw on Gus's wing. She felt as if her heart was full. They'd stopped Charlie and undone the harm he'd tried to do. And they'd done it all themselves, together.

Leaf darted forward. "If I can't have zero magic, then I want better magic!" Before anyone could say a word, he plunged his gecko face into the water. A few seconds later, he backed up. Droplets of water dripped from his face.

Poor Leaf, Holly thought. *He still doesn't understand.*

"Do you feel any different?" Zephyr asked.

Leaf squinched up his face in concentration, and then he expanded into a balloon and floated into the air. Hopping up, Bluebell caught him and pulled him back to earth. The rabbit transformed his hat into a bonnet with an abundance of ribbons and tied one of the ribbons around the gecko's back ankle.

"Why didn't it work?" the gecko wailed as he floated above them. "I'm not fixed!"

Gently, Holly said, "You weren't broken." She wished she could make him see. "The Moon Mirror couldn't change you, because it already did. It gave you its gift." They'd all been given their special magic. And Holly was sure: just because some wizards didn't think they fit with what was expected didn't mean there was anything wrong with them.

They were all powerful, each in their own way. It just took some of them — *like me,* Holly thought — a little longer to see that.

"But we fixed it!" Leaf said.

"Charlie lied," Gus told him. "He lied about everything. The

Moon Mirror didn't need fixing. It wasn't malfunctioning. That's just what he told us so he could work his spell on us. I don't think anything he said was true."

"He was a thief *and* a liar," Periwinkle agreed.

"I don't believe it!" Leaf cried.

Holly touched the water of the Moon Mirror with her paw. Ripples spread across the water. "This is the proof right here." As firmly, clearly, and gently as she could, she said to the little gecko, "The Moon Mirror was never broken. And neither were we."

Leaf's whole face drooped. Still floating, he made a soft hiccup-like cry. She'd never seen anyone look so miserable. "Then . . . it's over," he whimpered. "And I betrayed you for nothing. I thought . . . I thought . . . I'm so sorry!"

Zephyr scooted underneath him. "Hey, maybe . . . we can make things better without the Moon Mirror? Learn to use the ribbons." He picked up the one tied to the gecko's foot. "It'll work. I know it will. We can do it, together. You won't have to worry about the wind — I'll be your anchor, and you'll be my eyes."

"Can . . . can you forgive me?" Leaf asked.

"You're my best friend," Zephyr said. "Or . . . I thought you were." He pressed on. "I know you can be again."

The gecko deflated, drifting down to the ground beside Zephyr.

Holly wasn't sure that any of them would forget what Leaf had done, any more than they'd ever forget what Charlie had tried to do. Maybe with time, the little gecko would come to see he wasn't broken or a mistake or useless or powerless or anything but himself. And maybe then he'd be able to rebuild the trust he'd broken with her and the other shelterlings. Watching Leaf and Zephyr, she said, "I think it's time to go home."

"Home," Periwinkle said, as if trying out the word.

Holly put her paw around Periwinkle, as high as she could reach. "We have friends waiting for us." And their friends would all want to hear what had happened . . . and how everything was going to be okay. *It will be,* she thought. She was certain of that. In fact, she'd never felt so certain of anything in her life.

"Bluebell, can you make your ribbon hat?" Zephyr asked the rabbit.

"Absolutely!" Bluebell said, transforming his hat into the helmetlike sled. Zephyr picked up the ribbons in his mouth.

Clover knelt down on her two front legs. "Anyone who wants a cow-back ride, climb on." Periwinkle and Tangerine clambered onto the cow's back.

Bluebell raised his paw into the air. "A victory is twice itself when the winners return home," he proclaimed. "Come, my friends, it's time to leave."

Stepping onto the hat, Holly took up the ribbon reins. Bluebell climbed on with her, and, after a brief moment's hesitation, Leaf slunk on too. He curled his tail around himself and didn't meet their eyes, as if afraid they'd tell him he couldn't come, but no one said a word. As Clover began plodding down the mountain, Pepper and Gus flew on either side of her.

"Run, Zephyr," Holly told the turtle. "Take us home."

CHAPTER TWENTY-TWO

Holly and the others pulled by Zephyr reached the shelter first. She saw the white farmhouse and the blue trim, the porch with the nest, the trellis and the yard, and the pink peonies, and it all looked wonderful. She jumped off Bluebell's hat, scampered up to the porch, and ran in two tight circles.

She then ran inside. Everything was exactly where they'd left it — the pitcher that had once held the magic flower was still full of water, the footrest for the comfy armchair that Charlie favored was still positioned where he'd left it, the window where Clover had poked her head in was still open. Oddly, Holly felt like she'd been gone both for weeks and for no time at all.

As soon as everyone had returned and finished explaining everything to the shelterlings who'd stayed, she, Gus, and the others destroyed the flower, the herb, and the fruit and hid the other items around the shelter: in the kitchen cabinet, buried beneath the herb garden, in Periwinkle's room beneath her cache of stray lost things, and under the nest on the porch. By splitting up, they ensured that no one creature knew the fate of all seven items, and by destroying several of them, they guaranteed that even Periwinkle couldn't find them all. It was a group effort.

If Charlie ever returned, he'd never find them. *And we certainly won't help him again*, Holly thought.

Once everything was taken care of, the day continued as if it were just an ordinary day at the shelter, blending into two days and then three. Each day was as sunny and summery as the last. Clover grazed in the pasture. A few animals tended to the garden, helping one another pick the vegetables and carry them into the kitchen. Others prepared meals. The snakes napped in the sun, stretched out on a rock, and the bat slept upside down, hanging from one of the rafters in the barn.

From her perch on the nest on the porch, Holly watched Zephyr practice racing around the outside of the house, pulling Leaf on a ribbon, with Bluebell steering him around flowers and bushes. Gus sat beside her.

Floating high above the yard, Leaf seemed sad, she noticed, but Zephyr kept shouting encouragements. She hoped Leaf would be okay. And if he wasn't . . . well, maybe that wasn't up to her to fix. Leaf had to come to terms with who he was on his own. They could support him, but they couldn't walk his path for him. Everyone had to walk their own path.

Or fly. Or slither. Or whatever.

Watching them, Holly asked Gus, "How would you like to visit the ocean with me? I made a promise, and I intend to keep it."

"You can count on me, Holly," Gus said.

"Next week, then?" she suggested. "I think I'd like to be home awhile first, before our next adventure. But after that . . . I'd like to see the ocean again." And the mountains. And maybe a desert or a lake or a rainforest or . . .

"Sounds perfect," he said.

Pleased that that was settled, Holly went inside to check on the other shelterlings. Periwinkle was in her room, happily arranging her lost things, Tangerine was switching colors as he alternated between standing in front of the hall wallpaper and his bedroom wallpaper. In the living room, Strawberry was making all the furniture smell as pleasant as Cloud Mountain.

Everyone was where they were supposed to be . . . where they'd *chosen* to be.

✦

Two days later, Holly was sweeping the porch with her tail when Gus swooped down.

"Holly, the arrival circle! It's sparkling!"

"We didn't receive a letter," Holly said. Usually the familiars sent word, as they had with Periwinkle, so that the shelter could be prepared. "But that's okay." Everyone was always welcome here. They'd work together to find the right room for their new arrival.

She hurried with Gus to the circle of stones and waited while the purple cloud swirled and swirled. At last, a shape solidified in the center: a cat.

It was Saffron. "Hey, Holly, Gus. Good to see you again, under better circumstances. I take it you resolved your problem with your friend with the nasty spell?"

"Y-yes," Holly said.

While Gus and Holly stared at him, Saffron sauntered beneath the trellis onto the lawn as the purple cloud faded away. "So . . . is this the place?"

Gus recovered from his surprise first. "It's our home."

"The famous Shelter for Familiars," Saffron said.

"The Shelter for *Rejected* Familiars," Holly said. She said the word with pride. She'd rejected one life and chosen another. She was a shelterling and proud of it. "And I don't know that it's famous."

"Any chance it could also be the Shelter for *Former* Familiars?"

"Of course," Holly said immediately. "It's home for whoever needs it. But . . . *former* familiars?" She'd never heard of such a thing. Not that she was judging.

Saffron the former familiar sniffed the peonies. "You won your magic flower without a wizard, and you set out to face your traitorous friend without a single wizard, and that made me think that maybe *I* didn't need a wizard. So . . . here I am, wizardless and homeless, and hoping you have a space for me."

"Absolutely," Holly said.

She saw the muscles in Saffron's back relax. His fur settled down. *He was worried we'd say no*, she thought.

Even more firmly, Holly said, "All who want to be here are welcome."

"Very happy to hear it," Saffron said.

Holly patted the cat with her paw. "Come meet everyone. We have an array of residents here, and I'm sure you'll make lots of friends." She began to tell him about the other shelterlings: Clover, Bluebell, Periwinkle, Zephyr, Leaf . . .

Gus flew toward the windows and called inside, "We have a new shelterling!"

Everyone tumbled outside. Gathering around the cat, they all greeted him. "I'm Periwinkle! I'm new too!" Holly heard the lemur say. "Bluebell, at your service," the rabbit said.

Holly climbed onto the porch, and Gus landed beside her.

Together, they watched everyone chatter and laugh.

"You aren't nervous," Gus observed. "I think this is the first arrival day we've ever had where you weren't nervous about whether our new shelterling would like it here."

"I . . ." It was true. She didn't feel like running in circles or rushing to make sure the tablecloth was laid over the trough or the stray leaves were trimmed off the bushes. "For the first time, I feel like I don't need to prove this place is good enough. It's already wonderful exactly as it is, and if someone can't see that . . . well, I can't make them."

"I can see it," Gus said, "because of you."

"It wasn't me." She tried to find the right words. "I don't know how to make anyone be happy if they don't want to. All I can do is be the best *me* I can be."

"And that's enough," Gus said.

She watched the other shelterlings as they clustered around the cat. While Clover made pronouncements (in rhyme, of course) about what they'd have for dinner, Periwinkle offered to give their new arrival a tour. Saffron accepted, and Zephyr led the way, with Bluebell and Leaf helping. They all trooped up onto the porch and into the house.

"Yes, that's enough," Holly said at last.

And Holly and Gus followed their friends inside.

ACKNOWLEDGMENTS

So, I looked back at the very first notes I made for *The Shelterlings*, before I'd written a sentence of the story, even before I knew Holly was a squirrel, and found these two statements:

You're valuable, even if someone says you're not.

and

Include LOTS of talking animals.

Those two notes led to this book.

I've always secretly suspected that there is no story that cannot be improved by the addition of a talking animal, and with *The Shelterlings*, I had the joy, pleasure, and privilege of writing many. Thank you to my phenomenal editor, Anne Hoppe, who encouraged, guided, and inspired me throughout the process of writing this book, and to my amazing agent, Andrea Somberg, without whom none of my books would exist!

Thank you to Amanda Acevedo, Lisa DiSarro, Candace Finn, Emma Grant, Eleanor Hinkle, Samira Iravani, Marcie Lawrence, Mary Magrisso, Catherine Onder, Jackie Sassa, Helen Seachrist, John Sellers, Tara Shanahan, Karen Sherman, Kaitlin Yang, and all the other incredible people at Clarion Books and HarperCollins for bringing the story of Holly and her friends to life! And thank you to Brandon Dorman for the stunningly gorgeous cover art!

Much love and thanks to my magnificent and marvelous family, who had to deal with such questions as, "What's the most absurd magical power you can think of?" and "What's your favorite rodent?" at all hours. You are my heart, my world, and my life.

And an extra-special thank-you to my readers. Always remember: You are not a mistake. You are strong and powerful and important exactly as you are.

If you don't believe me, ask Holly.